FALCON
and the
CHARLES STREET
WITCH

FALCON
and the
CHARLES STREET
WITCH

Luli Gray

HOUGHTON MIFFLIN COMPANY
Boston 2002

www.houghtonmifflinbooks.com

The text of this book is set in Dante.

Library of Congress Cataloging-in-Publication Data

Gray, Luli.
    Falcon and the Charles Street Witch / Luli Gray.
        p. cm.
    Summary: Twelve-year-old Falcon must find the courage
to save the day—and the dragon, Egg—after having a series of
magical misadventures caused by her little brother, a distracted
old dragon, and a bumbling witch.
    ISBN 0-618-16410-3
    [1. Dragons—Fiction. 2. Witches—Fiction. 3. Magic—Fiction.
4. Courage—Fiction. 5. New York (N.Y.)—Fiction. 6. Australia—Fiction.]
I. Title

PZ7.G7794 Faj 2002
[Fic]—dc21
                                                    2001047058

Manufactured in the United States of America
QUM 10 9 8 7 6 5 4 3 2 1

For Bonnie Layman and Susie Wilde, friends indeed

With thanks to my agent, the (almost saintly)
George Nicholson,
to my intrepid editor,
Amy Flynn,
and to Jackie Ogburn, the voice of reason.

CHAPTER ONE

"I NEED TO GO NOW!" TOODY PRESSED HIS KNEES TOGETHER and tugged at Falcon's arm. Both toilets in the rear of the jumbo jet were OCCUPIED/OCCUPADO according to the sign on the doors. The plane was full, and now, at dawn, people were waking up, yawning, stretching to get the kinks out of their muscles after a night spent trying to sleep in their seats. Falcon could see that the toilets in the middle of the aircraft were just as crowded, and three other passengers were standing in line with her and her little brother. "Hold on for one minute, Tood," she said. "It's almost your turn." The smell of food drifting back from the galley made her stomach rumble. She rummaged in her fanny pack for LifeSavers, but they were all gone.

Falcon was glad to be going back to New York. It was fun riding around in her father's Land Rover, going to remote villages in the bush, and seeing kangaroos and koalas in the Outback, but now she was ready to go home. She had actually been pretty disappointed when Missy said they were going to spend Christmas with Peter in Australia and miss almost three months of school.

"Falcon, you know it's our turn to go to Peter's for the holidays. Anyhow, I thought you hated school," said Missy, running her hands through her wild hair. It was the beginning of a Deadline time, and Falcon knew her mother would be glad to have her and Toody away while she worked on her new book. "I thought you'd be glad to go."

"Why can't we go in June? We're starting journal writing after Christmas and Ms. Alberter got us these really cool journals from Kate's Paperie."

"Well, maybe next year—but everything's all arranged. You know that—we always do it this way. Come on, bird, Peter's going to take you to learn Aboriginal dancing and body painting. Oh, please don't roll your eyes, it is absolutely *maddening!*" Missy turned back to her easel, leaving Falcon to stomp out of the studio muttering, "I hate dancing."

Of course, once she was in Australia, she had a great time. Peter had a big, beautiful apartment in Sydney where they spent Christmas with Missy and several of her father's friends. He was a terrific cook, and the table looked like something out of *Gourmet* magazine, with crystal and silver that glittered in the candlelight. Missy looked so beautiful and Peter looked handsome, and she got to dress up and even wear a little lipstick and eye shadow.

"Powder and paint and perfume," sang Missy, dancing

around and spraying clouds of Pacific Midnight, her special smell of the week.

Falcon felt very grown up, and for once it was not her job to clean up the mess when Toody got bored and poured Missy's champagne into his milk.

After New Year's, Missy flew back to New York and Falcon, Toody, and Peter flew to Arnhem Land in the north, where Peter's Aboriginal friends lived. Peter was an ethnobotanist who studied the plants that native people use as medicine. He also spent a lot of time learning old ways of healing. He said that native shamans had a great deal of knowledge about medicine, especially about how important feelings and beliefs are in treating illness. Falcon wandered the forests with the young women, gathering food, while Toody played with the children and Peter talked with the healers.

But after three months in Australia, Falcon was homesick for New York. She especially missed her mother and Great-Great-Aunt Emily and Ardene Taylor, who would all be there to meet them at JFK Airport. She looked at her watch. They would be landing in less than four hours and she could hardly wait. Neither, apparently, could Toody. His face twisted in agony as he yanked at her sleeve. *"Now!"* he said.

Timidly, Falcon touched the shoulder of the large, bearded man at the front of the line.

"Excuse me, mister, could you please let my little brother go ahead of you? He really needs to go."

The man's yellow sweat suit was wrinkled and his face

was grumpy from the uncomfortable night he had spent in a seat that had obviously been designed by someone who had never had to sleep on a plane.

"Who doesn't?" he said, and turned his back. Later, witnesses said he grabbed at Toody as the little boy dashed past him and reached for the door. Some people thought he was trying to prevent the disaster, some said he just didn't want to give up his place in line. Either way, nobody would ever know. Toody threw his whole weight on the door handle just as Falcon and the others yelled "NO!" Falcon lunged at her brother, but her hands just brushed the back of his T-shirt and closed on empty air as she leapt after him, her own scream trailing behind her like a scarf. The last thing she saw was the red EXIT light glowing over the door as she and Toody and the angry man burst out of the plane in a blast of freezing wind. She rushed through the air as her brother tumbled head over heels below her, far out of reach, and vanished into a cloud. The other passenger, arms flailing, fell straight down, a bright yellow pinwheel against the sky.

Falcon thrashed against the freezing wind that tore her from her brother, but it was no use and the air was so cold! Behind her in the bucking plane a flight attendant clung to the back of a seat with Falcon's fanny pack dangling from her hand by its broken strap.

Falcon was sure she would freeze to death before she hit the ground. She supposed the plane must have crashed, though she couldn't see anything below but ocean, sky, and fat white clouds. She passed through one as she fell and was immediately drenched with icy rain. Now the wind felt much colder, and the water on her clothes and skin instantly turned to ice. *I'm a flying Popsicle,* she thought, and wondered why she wasn't screaming anymore. In fact she was getting sleepy, and a blackness began to close in around the edges of her vision. She thought she must be dying, and she felt sad that she would never again see Toody or Missy or Peter or Aunt Emily or . . .

The darkness was everywhere now, a fuzzy, sleepy darkness that must be death, not scary at all but soft and safe and deliciously warm against the blue goosebumps on her skin. Warm, so warm! Oh no, it was too warm, it was waking her up and now she would be awake when she crashed to Earth and smashed into a million pieces. She opened her mouth to scream but the scream never came. She had stopped falling! The darkness was gone and she saw blue sky all around and sea below, with a patch of brown land in the distance. She was floating on a warm current of air, floating down as gently and slowly as dandelion fluff. The warm wind had dried her clothes and hair and blown away the dark sleep of death, and she found she could move or lie or sit on her flying carpet of air. She was descending so slowly that she had time to look around.

The patch of land grew bigger, and now she saw clumps of green here and there, though most of the land was brownish gray. She wondered whether she was approaching New York, and if those flashes of light were the sun reflecting off the windows in a thousand skyscrapers.

A pair of bright black-and-yellow eyes appeared suddenly right in front of her face. The sea gull squawked as it stalled in midair to avoid crashing into her. Flapping wildly, it regained its balance and flew off, crying, *Gah! gah! gah!* It was not at all accustomed to seeing twelve-year-old girls in jeans and red sneakers flying over the ocean.

Falcon watched the gull as it swooped down toward the landmass, graceful again, flying with scarcely a flicker of its wings. She stuck her arms out and flapped as hard as she could, searching the sky for any sign of Toody, but it made no difference, she had no control over her descent. As she floated closer to the land, the air current grew stronger and warmer and she began to slow down. She wondered what the source of the friendly wind might be and remembered how in one of the Narnia stories Aslan's warm breath floated the children safely down from a high cliff. But of course that was just a fairy tale. This must be some sort of weird oceanic weather. She knew there were all sorts of strange winds in the world with names like chinook, pampero, mistral, and sirocco—maybe this was one of them.

She hoped Toody had been caught by the wind, too. Maybe he was down there somewhere! Maybe she could find him; with Peter, Missy, Aunt Emily, and Ardene Taylor, not to mention the New York Police Department, she could probably find anyone. Falcon peered down at the Earth below but couldn't make out any familiar landmarks. Was it New York? Or was it Sydney or Melbourne or some other place? And how would she find her way home? She panicked for a moment before she remembered that she could phone home from almost anywhere in the world. *But how will I land*, she wondered. *I'm not slowing down anymore and I still have no control.* She supposed she ought to worry, but the air was soft and warm and she felt so safe. The soft sound of the wind and the warm cushion of air beneath her made her sleepy again, and though she struggled to keep her eyes open, her eyelids drooped more and more till she fell fast asleep.

CHAPTER
TWO

FALCON WOKE UP SUDDENLY AS SHE LANDED WITH A gentle bump on a green lawn. She looked around, wondering where she could be. The lawn, she saw, was part of a garden surrounded by a high stone wall covered in lilacs. A tall cherry tree grew on one side, its branches spreading a canopy of pink blossoms over one corner of the lawn, and a doghouse, painted blue and white, stood nearby. A sign over the entrance said, BEWARE OF THE MANTICORE. Falcon stood up and turned to see a cottage, painted in the same colors as the doghouse, with a bright blue door that opened as she watched. A small, plump woman dressed in a blue-and-white-checked dress stepped out. She carried a large tray set with a blue teapot, two teacups painted with forget-me-nots, two blue napkins, and two plates that matched the cups. The woman walked down the path, set the tray on the grass, and smiled at Falcon.

"Whoosha! That was heavy. Well, so you're here at last, my dear. Come help me fetch the rest of our tea. . . . I'm sure you're hungry after your long flight."

Falcon didn't move and her mouth hung open as she stared at the odd little woman, who seemed to be expecting her, which was impossible. The woman went back into the house and came out again with a plate in each hand.

"Now then, dearie, more to come." Falcon, still staring, stood up and took the plates, setting them down on the grass next to the tea tray. One plate held six chocolate cupcakes covered in blue-and-white icing, and the other held a pile of dainty sandwiches. The little woman emerged again with two more plates in her hands and a saucer of lemon wedges on her head. She arranged all the plates on the lawn and sat down cross-legged, patting the grass next to her and smiling up at Falcon.

"Sit down and eat, my dear," she said.

"Who—?" said Falcon. "Where am—"

"Time enough; tea first," said her hostess, and she poured out two cups. Falcon realized she was starving after who knows how many hours flying through the air, and no breakfast before that. She began with the sandwiches (cucumber, watercress, tomato, ham, egg salad, chicken, and smoked salmon) and went on to cupcakes, raspberry jam puffs, and cheese tartlets. At last she sat back and watched the little woman pour her a second cup of tea. She added milk and two lumps of sugar and handed it to Falcon, interrupting her just as she opened her mouth to speak.

"There! Never ask questions on an empty stomach, I always say. Now, my dear, I am Blinda C-h-o-l-m-o-n-d-e-l-y, pronounced Chumley, and you are in my garden, on Charles Street in New York City."

Falcon opened her mouth to protest. She had lived in New York City all her life and this didn't look like anyplace she had ever seen. Then she looked more carefully and saw that brick buildings towered all around the garden beyond the wall. When she sniffed the air, it had the familiar New York smell that is a mixture of car fumes, river water, hot dogs, tar, and the mingled odors of eight million human beings all mixed up together.

"How did you know I was coming?" she asked.

"I'm a witch, of course," said Ms. Cholmondely, pronounced Chumley, licking blue icing off her thumb. Falcon stared at her. All she could think of were Glinda's words to Dorothy in *The Wizard of Oz*, so she said them.

"Are you a good witch or a bad witch?" At this Blinda's face turned beet red and she spilled tea all over her skirt.

"Oh, drat!" she said, and mopped at herself with a napkin. Falcon thought she must have asked the wrong question and wondered rather nervously whether Blinda was embarrassed because she *was* a bad witch. She certainly didn't look bad, like the Wicked Witch of the West. She was round and pretty, with silver-streaked brown hair in long braids wound untidily around her head and bright brown eyes behind a pair of tortoiseshell glasses whose stems were mended with tape. And the tea had been both generous and delicious. Falcon couldn't believe that a bad witch would be such a good cook. At last Blinda Cholmondely stopped flapping the napkin over her skirt and raised both her chins with a slightly defiant air.

"I'm neither good nor bad, of course. A silly question, I always think. Even Glinda isn't always good, and I say it though she is my third cousin thrice removed. As for me, I'm a . . . pretty good witch, most of the time. So there!"

Falcon didn't quite understand but she felt reassured. After all, she herself was a pretty good girl, and that was okay. Then she remembered that Toody was lost or maybe even dead and that she hadn't taken good care of him at all. What would Missy say? What would Peter and Aunt Emily say? For a moment she seemed to feel the smooth warmth of her brother's skin and hear his delighted giggles as he sat curled in her lap while she read *Green Eggs and Ham*. It always made him laugh, no matter how often she read it. She bit her lip and looked at Blinda, who was eating the last jam puff to calm herself.

"My brother," said Falcon, "he fell out and I couldn't catch him and he's gone. Oh, Ms. Cholmondely, I have to find him. Can you help me?"

The witch stood up and pulled Falcon to her feet. Then she looked at the mess of dishes and food scraps on the lawn, pointed her finger, and said, "Clean up!" At once there was a great whirling and clattering as cups, plates, and spoons went flying through the open door of the cottage with the teapot and milk jug trundling after and the napkins flapping like big blue bats overhead. The food scraps all flew up onto the wall and made themselves into crumbs for the birds, and a sound of running water and splashing came from the house as the tea things washed themselves up. Falcon almost forgot her troubles in delight at this convenient way to do housework. "That's really amazing!" she said to Blinda. The witch patted her hair modestly and smiled.

"Pretty good, if I say it myself," she said, and led the way into the cottage.

Inside it looked to Falcon like a hobbit's house, though not a very tidy one. The furniture was smaller than regular furniture and it looked homemade and a bit shabby. There were bright rag rugs on the floor and jam jars full of lilacs, forsythia, and cherry blossoms on every available surface. Two white bookcases stood in the living room; one was filled with volumes on cooking and gardening, while the other held the complete works of Stephen King in hardcover, a boxed set of *Alice in Wonderland* and *Through the Looking Glass*, *Roget's Thesaurus*, a well-thumbed copy of *Magic Potions on a Budget*, an illustrated three-volume set of *Spells for All Occasions*, and a stack of *Every Witchway: The Sorcerer's Quarterly* with a crystal ball weighing it down. An old-fashioned black dial telephone stood on the table in front of the couch, which had been slipcovered—not very skillfully—in pale yellow cotton. An enormous orange cat sat squarely in the middle, staring disapprovingly at Falcon.

"Augustus, meet Falcon Davies," said Blinda Cholmondely.

Humph, said the cat, and he turned his back on them
both.

"So rude," said the witch. "Don't you think you
should phone your mother?"

Falcon sat on a small hassock next to the sofa, picked
up the phone, and dialed the first three numbers. Then
she stopped and turned to Blinda. "Toody," she said.
"What will I tell her?"

Instead of answering, Blinda took Falcon's arm and
sniffed it. "Just as I thought," she said. "Dragonsbreath,
and a young one at that, still on cod liver oil. And you're
wearing the ring." Falcon looked blank. The witch sighed
and sat down next to the cat, taking the phone out of
Falcon's hand.

"Really, my dear, you're not too swift, are you? You
wear a ring made of moonsilver and forged in dragonfire,
and that smell tells me you got here on dragonsbreath. If
I'm any judge, Toody probably got picked up, too, though
where he is now I couldn't say at the moment."

"Dragonsbreath?" said Falcon, her eyes lighting up.
"You mean Egg? Egg saved us?"

"Don't know about 'us,' can't be sure. It was the One
you call Egg, though that's not her real name, of course."

Falcon stared at Blinda, her mind racing. When Egg
flew off into the night more than a year before, she was
sure she would never see her dragon again. It had taken

all her courage and love to let Egg go then, not knowing what would happen to her, but knowing what might. Captured by scientists who would keep her in a cage or do experiments on her; shot down by hunters who would mount her beautiful seahorse head on a trophy room wall; or gone to some bleak and lonely place where there would be no one to love her.

Missy had been so kind at first, telling Falcon how brave she was to let Egg go, and how proud she was. Then, after a while, she began to change the subject whenever Falcon talked about dragons.

"A little magic is all very well, Falcon, but it's over now and you have to live in the real world, go to school, make friends."

"But Egg *is* real, as real as, as . . . *socks!*" said Falcon, who was folding laundry at the time. Her mother turned to leave the room.

"Throw out the holey ones, would you, bird? I've got to get some work done."

Falcon tried talking to Ardene Taylor. It had been at least four months since they'd had tea together. Ardene answered the door but didn't open it all the way.

"Oh, hello, Falcon," she said. "Is everything all right?"

"Yes. I mean no. I . . ." She began again. "Can I come in? Missy has a Deadline, and she . . ." She gulped and looked up at her friend's kind face. Ardene sighed.

"Oh, Falcon, I'm afraid I have a Deadline, too, with my NYU course and the new book and . . . oh, look, hon, what do you say I take a short break and we'll have some tea, okay?" Falcon nodded and stepped into Ardene's sunny apartment. In no time she was sitting on the sofa drinking tea out of a chipped mug. A milk carton stood next to a saucer that held the used tea bags, and there wasn't any sugar. Stacks of paper lay on every surface with Post-it Notes stuck on the top pages, and Ardene did not look like her usual elegant self. She was wearing sweats and her hair was pulled back with a rubber band. She plunked herself down in the armchair next to Falcon, handed her a box of Lorna Doones, and took a big gulp of tea.

"Oh, that tastes good," she said. "I'm glad you came by, dear, I'm working much too hard these days. Cookie?"

"No thank you, Ardene. I wanted to talk about Egg." Ardene smiled and touched the scorch mark on the arm of her chair.

"A memento of magic," she said. "Wasn't that a time? My goodness, more than a year ago—the time goes so fast. Have you made any new friends this year?"

Falcon had, in fact, and she was much happier at Chapman than she had been before. She was friends with most of the kids in her Advanced Reading class and there was a new girl, Allie Newton, who liked the Museum of Natural History as much as she did. She took a cookie and bit into it, though she wasn't hungry.

"I'm sort of making friends, only I really miss Egg, Ardene. Remember how she used to—"

Ardene stood up and gave Falcon a quick hug.

15

"Egg was lovely, sweetie, and I know how you must miss her. We'll have a really good talk soon, shall we? After the New Year." She smiled at Falcon as she led her to the door.

"Right now *my* job is to design my course and finish my new book, and *your* job is to go to school and make friends and have some fun, for heaven's sake! Try writing down what's on your mind, why don't you?" She touched Falcon's cheek with her hand. "Okay?" she said, and shut the door.

Falcon had tried writing down her thoughts and memories of Egg in letters to her father in Australia. At first he loved hearing about her finding the big scarlet egg in Central Park, the story of the hatching, the dangerous walks after midnight with the baby dragon as she grew bigger and hotter. He wrote back to say how much he was enjoying the letters.

"Your stories are wonderful, bird. Maybe you'll be a writer someday," he wrote. Falcon put that one in her treasure box. But later, when she took it out to reread, the word "stories" popped out at her. Did Peter think she had made it all up? She wasn't sure.

Great-Great-Aunt Emily was always happy to listen. But it had been so long since Egg had flown away, and the more Falcon talked about her, the more like a fairy story she seemed to be. The ring on Falcon's finger was just metal and the piece of eggshell in her treasure box had faded to a dull orange. Toody was perfectly willing to talk about Egg, but he didn't seem to care whether she was truth or fantasy. The dragon was no more or less real to him than the bears and monsters in his own dreams.

Now here was this odd little woman talking about dragonsbreath in the most matter-of-fact way, as though magic were an everyday thing. Maybe Blinda could help her find Toody. It would prove to Peter that her stories were true, and that there was more to her than fairy tales and good spelling. Her brain felt like it had a hurricane inside it with too many ideas and possibilities all blowing and roaring through at once. It made her dizzy. She put one hand on either side of her head to hold it steady. *I'll go home and tell them*, she thought. *The magic is real and we can use it to find Toody!* She picked up the phone again and dialed. After three rings her mother's voice said, "Hello?"

"Missy," said Falcon, "it's me. I'm home."

CHAPTER
THREE

THE NEXT THREE DAYS WERE A CONFUSING WHIRL THAT made Falcon feel like a small bird flying through a cyclone. When her cab got to 16 West 77th Street, Missy and Ardene Taylor were waiting on the sidewalk to meet her, and there was a lot of hugging and crying. A kind woman from the Federal Aviation Authority came by with two plainclothes detectives from the New York Police Department to question Falcon about the accident. She told them almost everything but said nothing about dragons or witches or dishes that washed themselves. She was pretty sure they wouldn't believe her. As it turned out, they didn't seem to believe what she *did* tell them; she saw them exchanging glances when she got to the part about floating down to Earth on a warm air current.

Lieutenant Eddler sat in the kitchen with Falcon while she made him a cup of tea. The others were talking with Missy in the living room.

"Thanks, Falcon. That's great, just two sugars," said Lieutenant Eddler. "Now then, maybe you can tell me, or show me, what you were doing when the emergency exit opened."

"Standing in line for the bathroom," said Falcon, wondering why he was asking this again.

"Oh yeah, I know, but I mean, when it opened and you jumped out after your brother, what position were you in, exactly?"

Falcon tried to remember. She stretched her arms out, leaning forward with her legs wide apart so her body formed an X.

"Like that," she said. "I was trying to grab him." The lieutenant nodded, rubbing his chin with one hand. He picked up his tea and went back into the living room. Ms. Ortiz from the FAA came in and Falcon made tea for her, too, while Ms. Ortiz asked her about the emergency exit.

"Did it look normal to you, Falcon?" she said. *Normal?* What did that mean? Falcon took a carton of milk out of the refrigerator.

"I don't know," she said. "It looked fine, I don't know what it looked like." Her hand shook, spilling milk onto the table, and her eyes filled with tears.

"I should've grabbed him, I should've been paying attention!" Ms. Ortiz was on her feet in a minute with her arm around Falcon.

"No, no. It's okay, honey, it wasn't your fault, we're just trying to figure out what happened. It's okay."

"I told you!" said Falcon, her voice coming out in a

muffled squeak. "It was a warm wind, it held me up, but Toody, I couldn't get him. He just fell down and down." She began to cry hard against Ms. Ortiz's blue suit jacket and Missy came in, her own face streaked with tears.

"That's enough," she said, pulling Falcon away. "She's told you all she knows. Go on, bird, you go lie down. I'm going to wash my face. I'll be in soon." She went into the bathroom.

As Falcon went to her room she heard Lieutenant Eddler say, "Skydiving position, she woulda floated right down, skinny kid like that. Prob'ly blacked out when she hit the water and someone picked her up. Maybe a drug runner's boat—they'd a just dumped her on shore and split."

"Posttraumatic stress," said Ms. Ortiz. "She can't really remember much, poor baby. What about the brother, though, and the big guy, Bender?"

"Not a chance," said Eddler in a low voice. "Poor kid."

Falcon slammed her door and flopped on the bed.

"Stupid, stupid, stupid," she muttered, punching the pillow. She stayed there till everyone had gone but Missy and Ardene.

Peter arrived soon after the policemen and the FAA lady left, and he hugged Falcon so hard she was nearly squished. Falcon was surprised to learn that her journey through the air had lasted more than twenty-four hours, so that by the time she phoned her mother from Blinda Cholmondely's house, Missy was frantic and Peter was on his way to New York from Sydney. Apparently the plane had not crashed, though several people had been bruised and shaken by the turbulence that followed the opening of the emergency exit. The pilot was able to land the plane in Los Angeles and there the passengers were questioned about the accident. Both Peter and Missy said again and again that it wasn't her fault about Toody, but their faces looked so sad when they spoke of him that she could hardly bear it.

She told them and Ardene about dragonsbreath and Blinda, but they just looked uncomfortable and wouldn't meet her eyes.

"Oh, darling bird," said Missy, "we'd all like to think that Toody . . ." She gulped and wiped her eyes. "That Toody managed to survive as miraculously as you did, and of course the police and the FBI and the FAA are all looking for him, and for poor Mr. Bender, too. But Egg is long gone; you have to let go of that, my bird. And I've lived in New York all my life; there's no such house on Charles Street, truly there isn't."

Falcon stared at her parents as though they were strangers and turned to Ardene as she came in with a tray of soup and toast to keep everyone's strength up. Falcon could see by her face that she didn't want to talk about Egg either. She wished Freddy Maldonado were there; he was a scientist and wouldn't deny the reality of Egg. But he was away on a birding expedition in South America and wouldn't be back for months. Was she all alone among the grownups?

There were only four weeks of school left, so, to her

21

relief, Falcon was allowed to continue with the home-schooling program she had been on since Christmas instead of going back to Chapman. Great-Great-Aunt Emily offered to tutor her since Missy and Peter were too involved with the search for Toody and the investigation of the accident. Ardene would work with her on math, of which Aunt Emily said, "It is a mystery to me beyond the times table."

Ten days after her return Falcon walked across the park to Aunt Emily's apartment. She was glad to get away from 4B, where every phone call made her parents jump, and every reminder of Toody made her mother cry. It was a gorgeous April morning and the wind seemed to blow her worries away, at least for the moment. She took the elevator up to her great-great-aunt's apartment and rang the bell. As usual she had a long wait before Emily, leaning on her silver-topped cane, opened the door.

"Ah, Falcon," she said. "Come in and we'll tackle *Moby Dick*."

Falcon got through Language Arts and Social Studies in record time, and by twelve-thirty she was devouring cheese and tomato sandwiches at Emily's long dining room table, wondering what whale steak would taste like. Emily poured her another glass of milk and sat back, sipping her own milk and watching her great-great-niece finish the last sandwich. She took a grape from the silver epergne and nibbled it thoughtfully, staring into space, gathering her thoughts.

"I know Blinda Cholmondely," she said. Falcon

stopped eating and stared, her eyes wide. "We're old friends," Emily went on. "I met her in 1900, when she came to work in my parents' house. She was my nanny, and later we went to France together in 1917, with the nursing corps. It was so horrible, that war. Blinda hated it even more than I did, and she tried so hard to keep people from getting hurt. Once, just before a skirmish, she turned all the soldiers' guns to chocolate." Aunt Emily grinned, remembering. "She didn't mean to, of course, she only meant to make them misfire, but she has such a sweet tooth, and her spells got muddled. You should have seen their faces when those evil-looking guns began to melt in their hands. The whole village smelled of Hershey bars!"

Falcon did some quick figuring in her head. "But that was more than eighty years ago! Ms. Cholmondely doesn't look that old—she hardly even has any wrinkles."

"Oh, she's young for a witch, about four hundred years old, I think—early middle age really. Why, her grandmother Ninda lived to be over a thousand; now *she* was a truly talented witch. The Cholmondelys have been around since the Stone Age, you know. And Falcon, they know all about dragons." She smiled at her niece.

"Why don't Missy and Peter believe me about Egg and Blinda? Even Ardene! She knew Egg from the beginning and she doesn't believe me either; I know she doesn't."

The old lady set down her glass and patted her lips with a napkin.

"I am very old, Falcon, and you are still young. We

know what the important things are: the way the air smells just before it rains, the creatures that live in the corners of dark rooms, the spinning wheel of sky overhead when you lie on your back in the grass on a summer day. We care about the taste of ice-cold milk with a chocolate chip cookie, and the smell of your mother's neck when she tucks you in at night. When we're born, we know there's magic in the world. Then we grow up and grow afraid of things we can't explain, but if we're smart and lucky we remember what's important when we get old, as I have. Some folks, like Blinda, never forget."

"I won't forget," said Falcon, clenching her fists. "Never!"

Emily did not reply. After a while she said, "Well then, shall we go and find Toody?"

She said it so casually, as though she were suggesting a walk to the corner for ice cream, but the question hit Falcon like a lightning bolt. She jumped up from her chair, knocking it over in her excitement.

"You mean you know where he is?"

"No," said Emily. "But among the three of us we should be able to find him. Blinda and I are quite sure he's alive and that Egg is mixed up in it somehow. Shall we go?"

CHAPTER
FOUR

DOWNTOWN ON CHARLES STREET, FALCON AND AUNT Emily walked along until they smelled the fresh scent of lilacs. The street seemed to shake itself and suddenly, right there in front of them, was the high stone wall draped with pale purple blossoms. There was no gate to be seen and they were just about to look around the corner when a voice said, "Here you are! I've been waiting. Come in, come in!" and there was Blinda Cholmondely in a pink-checked dress, beckoning to them from a curlicued iron gate that had certainly not been there a minute before.

They stepped through into the garden, where, Falcon was surprised to see, the doghouse and the cottage were now painted pink and white, and the sign over the doghouse read BEWARE OF THE BASILISK.

They followed Blinda into the cottage and sat down in

the living room, where Augustus lay draped over the hassock in a magnificent and disdainful manner.

Blinda Cholmondely set a pitcher of pink lemonade and a plate of oatmeal cookies on the table and sat down, taking Falcon's hand.

"Now then, my dear," she said, "tell us exactly what you saw of Toody after you all fell out of the airplane."

It was a great relief to tell the truth and know she would be believed. Falcon shut her eyes, trying to visualize every detail of the accident. She began to describe everything, from the freezing chill of the stratosphere to the sight of yellow Mr. Bender plummeting straight down, to Toody tumbling head over heels into a great fluffy white cloud.

"I never saw him after that and then I blacked out," she said, opening her eyes. She wiped a tear from her cheek and took a deep shaky breath.

Blinda got up and dragged over a small TV set that stood on a rickety cart in a corner of the room. She put her hands on her plump hips and looked around.

"Now, let's see," she said. "Where did I put that remote?" She began searching the bookshelves and lifting the piles of newspapers and magazines that lay on the table. Falcon wondered why she wanted to watch television now. She didn't see how that could help them find Toody, and she was rather disappointed in the witch after all the amazing things Aunt Emily had said about Blinda's magic.

Blinda pulled at the sofa cushions Falcon and Aunt

Emily were sitting on. "I know it's around here somewhere," she muttered.

The big orange cat heaved himself up, arched his
back, and said, "Freezer." He yawned, showing a set of
sharp white teeth, and leapt to the top of a bookcase.
Blinda went into the kitchen and came back waving the
remote control triumphantly. She pointed it at the TV and
it clicked onto a picture of a man rolling out a pie crust.
He was talking but no sound came out.

"Drat!" said Blinda and stuck a wooden chopstick into
the volume control.

" . . . gluten, relax by chilling before
you bake," roared the chef, making them all jump.
Blinda fiddled with the chopstick until the sound was
reduced to a bearable level. She pointed the remote and
clicked the channel changer, but all that happened was
that the image on the screen split into four quarters, each
one showing the mustachioed chef, now filling a pie shell
with blueberries.

"Tapioca," he said, "sugar, a little lemon zest, like so."

Blinda Cholmondely kept clicking the remote but
all she got was blueberry pies and more blueberry pies.
Augustus jumped down from the bookcase, landing
with a thud on the rag rug. He ambled over to the TV,
leapt up, and settled himself like a leopard on a tree limb,
his enormous fluffy tail hanging down over the screen
like a windshield wiper.

Immediately the screen filled with swirling multicolored lines that cleared to reveal a bright blue sky studded

with fluffy white clouds. As they watched, the clouds began to move faster and faster till all of a sudden Falcon cried, "Toody!"

There he was, floating in midair as the cloud he had fallen into was blown away. The little boy tumbled slowly head over heels through the sky for ten feet and then seemed to land on an invisible trampoline, where he bounced up and down for several minutes with a surprised look on his face before settling onto the air current that supported him. He looked around, flapped his arms, and kicked his legs in a swimming motion. At last he stood up, unzipped his shorts, and peed over the edge of the current. He stepped back, sat down, searched his pockets, and pulled out a half-eaten granola bar. Picking off most of the lint, he sat munching until the bar was gone, then he curled up on the air and went to sleep. At this point the screen went zigzaggy and cleared to show Julia Child making an amazing mess with a potful of sugar syrup and a broom handle.

"Just wave it around," she said in her flutey voice, "and soon you'll have a lovely spun sugar cage for your—" The image changed again to a young woman in a chef's toque tying up a chicken with string and talking without any sound.

"Really, Blinda, you should never have subscribed to that Food Network," said Aunt Emily. Blinda Cholmondely put down the remote and pointed her finger at the television.

"Asga figgle, hoggly woody, show us now just where is Toody!"

Augustus's tail swept across the screen, erasing the tied-up chicken to show Toody, still asleep, descending into a dry, brown landscape dotted here and there with eucalyptus trees. In the distance stood a . . . what? Falcon couldn't make it out, though it looked vaguely familiar. Green and red, glossy and long-tailed, with large leathery wings edged in gold—could it be? It was!

"Egg!" she cried. "It's Egg!"

CHAPTER
FIVE

I T *WAS* EGG, VERY MUCH LARGER THAN SHE HAD BEEN
when she flew off into the night more than a year
before. The dragon was now as big as a horse, and her
turquoise eyes sparkled like jewels as she blew out the
steady stream of warm air that supported Toody till he
landed gently right in front of her.

"Hello, Egg," he said.

The dragon gazed down at the little boy and said,
"Well met by sunlight, Tudor Davies."

"She can talk!" said Falcon.

"Well, of course she can, all dragons can by the time
they're two. Didn't you?" Blinda sat by the TV, ready to
adjust the chopstick in case the volume went out of control again. She looked very pleased with herself now that
things were working properly.

On the TV, Toody and Egg were walking together

across the dry brown land, Toody keeping a safe distance from the dragon's heat.

"When you were at home," Egg was saying, "you were in a better place, but travelers must be content."

"Where are we going?" asked Toody, who had to run a few steps every so often to keep up with the dragon's swift waddle.

"Once more onto the beach, dear friend," said Egg, pausing to strike a dramatic pose, one claw on her chest, the other pointing straight ahead.

"She seems to speak entirely in mangled quotations from Shakespeare," said Great-Great-Aunt Emily, peering closely at the screen.

"That's always the problem with dragons, and the Old Ones are worse; they misquote Euripides," said Blinda, taking another cookie.

The dragon and the little boy were now just visible as a big blob and a small blob on the horizon. After a moment they vanished, leaving the three watchers staring at the arid landscape.

"If Egg saved us, why didn't she bring us both to the same place?" asked Falcon.

"I expect it's because she couldn't," said Blinda. "She's still very young and inexperienced, you know, and dragons-breath flight is extremely difficult, even for the Old Ones."

"Then where are they?" asked Falcon. Blinda Cholmondely looked up at the ceiling, but apart from a few cobwebs she found nothing there.

"Spell," said Augustus, blinking his green eyes.

"Just so, just so," said the witch, and she began rummaging in a large Bloomingdale's shopping bag that stood by the bookcase.

"Now, let's see . . . lost key spells, lost earring spells, lost sock spells . . . aha! Lost boy spells!" She waved a scrap of paper and went into the kitchen, where they heard her crashing around in drawers and cupboards. She came back with a small saucepan in one hand and a plastic bag in the other. She put a potholder on the table and set the saucepan on top. Then out of the bag she took a broken compass, a handful of gray feathers, a jar of raspberry jam, and a tiny bottle of gin, the kind they serve on airplanes. She spread jam over the compass, put it in the bottom of the saucepan, and arranged the feathers over it.

"Homing pigeon," she said, looking up from the feathers. "At least I think they are—my files seem to have got a bit muddled somehow." She sprinkled gin over the things in the pot.

Aunt Emily was looking more and more anxious.

"Blinda, are you sure this is the right spell? You remember what happened with the cab driver and the fruit bat. . . ."

"Yes, yes, yes!" said Blinda Cholmondely. "I've told you a million times, it was just the wrong sort of bat! How was I to know it meant baseball bat? There's no mistake here: compass, homing pigeon feathers, jam. All boys like jam, you know. Here goes!"

She lit a match and dropped it into the saucepan. With

a whoosh the mixture flared up, sending flames nearly to the ceiling before they subsided with a good deal of smoke and a strong smell of burnt feathers. Blinda opened a window and poured everyone some lemonade while the contents of the pot cooled off. Falcon looked inside. The pot was empty except for seven shiny red letters that formed the mysterious word ARAFURA.

Blinda reached in, picked up the *A*, and handed it to Falcon. It was slightly sticky and smelled of raspberries.

"Eat it," said the witch. Falcon looked dubiously at the small red *A* in her hand. She didn't really want to eat anything made out of pigeon feathers and old compass parts. But Aunt Emily and Blinda were waiting, and she was sure her great-great-aunt wouldn't let her eat anything that would hurt her. She shut her eyes, put the *A* in her mouth, and bit down. To her surprise, it was delicious, and she ate it right up. The moment she swallowed, a wide blue-green ocean bordered by golden sand appeared behind her closed eyes. Tall trees grew inland, and she smelled pine and the Noxzema scent of eucalyptus. As she watched from behind her eyelids, Egg and Toody stepped out of the forest onto the beach. When Toody saw the blue waves lapping on the shore, he shouted and ran ahead of the dragon, shedding clothes as he ran. He plunged naked into the water and splashed happily while the dragon kept her distance. After a while Toody came out of the water, pulled on his shorts, and looked up at Egg.

"Can we go home now?" he said.

Egg stared at the little boy, and then her eyes shifted

and she began to chew her left foretalon. After a moment she said, "Let you not dwell on this base island by some spell, but release you from these bands with the help of Falcon's hands."

Toody spun around, looking in all directions. "Falcon?" he called. "Is she here?"

Egg turned so that she was face to face with Falcon. She actually seemed to be staring into her eyes, as though she could see her.

"Come unto these yellow sands and let's take hands. Come hither, come hither, come hither." With that the scene went dark, and the dragon's words echoed in Falcon's head. She opened her eyes to see her aunt and the witch staring at her as she leapt up from her chair.

"I saw them! They're on a beach and Egg told me to come! I have to go find them! Oh, please help me, Ms. Cholmondely!"

"A beach, an ocean . . . Blinda, where is your atlas?" Aunt Emily's voice calmed Falcon, and looking in the atlas seemed like a sensible thing to do. Blinda muttered, "Atlas, atlas," to herself, searching the bookcase. "Sofa!" she said, and flopped down on her stomach to pull the large blue volume out from under the couch. She set it on the table in front of Aunt Emily, who turned to the index.

"Aracuai, Arad, Arada, Arafura Sea! That's it, B5 page 50! Here it is, the Arafura Sea, in Australia."

They studied the map. The Arafura Sea lay on the north side of Australia and included a large area from

Darwin in the west to Cape York in the east. Falcon looked at the scale at the bottom of the page and measured the Arafura Sea with her thumb and forefinger.

"Six hundred miles!" she said. "How will I ever know where to look?"

"Don't give up before you start, child," said Emily.

Blinda left the room and came back carrying an object Falcon didn't recognize. She unfolded it and pushed a button on one side. It was a small seat, like a bicycle seat set on a short, rubber-tipped pole that, as Blinda demonstrated, could be lengthened or shortened at the push of a button.

"Shooting stick," said Blinda. "For taking on hunting expeditions." She set the rubber tip on the floor, adjusted the length, and sat down on the seat, looking smug. Unfortunately, either she was too heavy for the seat or the mechanism hadn't locked properly, because with a loud *sprong!* the pole suddenly collapsed, dumping Blinda onto the floor.

"Oh, drat and double drat!" said the witch. Falcon bit her lip to keep from laughing.

Blinda untangled herself from the shooting stick and fiddled with the button. "Just needs a bit of oil, I expect. Much better than a broomstick, you see, folds up small when you don't want it, and you always have a place to sit—so handy." She smiled triumphantly.

"Blinda," said Aunt Emily patiently, "Falcon isn't a witch, she's a human girl. She can't ride a shooting stick.

She'll have to go to Australia by plane. Unless we can think of a better way."

Blinda Cholmondely turned red with embarrassment. "Oh, I forgot. Sorry, not your fault. Human, oh dear." She and Aunt Emily began to discuss possibilities.

Falcon didn't listen because she was wondering what Missy and Peter would say when she told them she wanted to go looking for Toody in Australia. She was trying to think of some good arguments when Blinda said, "This should do it, if I've used the right sort of snail." She handed Falcon a cardboard box labeled SLOW FOOD.

"Put it in their cereal tomorrow morning. They'll never know you've gone."

Falcon looked doubtfully at the box and shook it. It made a dry, rustling sound.

"Oh, Blinda, are you sure?" said Aunt Emily.

"Of course I am, Emily, must you question my every spell? This is the very best quality. It will affect twenty blocks north and south at the most, and crosstown, no more."

"But Rhode Island . . ."

"That wasn't my fault, there was a gale-force wind. Trust me, dear, it's *quite* safe." The witch smirked at Emily and patted Falcon's shoulder.

Falcon thanked Blinda and left the cottage (which was now painted yellow and white), walked past the doghouse (BEWARE OF THE HIPPOGRIFF), and stepped through the gate in the wall with her aunt. Emily waved her cane to hail a cab, and when they got in, she patted Falcon's shoulder and said, "Don't worry, Falcon, Blinda Cholmondely's potions never do any harm, though they don't always work exactly as expected. Do as she told you and come up to the roof of my building at eight o'clock tomorrow morning."

"How can I . . ." said Falcon. But her great-great-aunt had fallen asleep, as very old people sometimes do, and she didn't wake up even when the cab dropped Falcon off at number 16 and drove off toward East 66th Street.

CHAPTER
SIX

MISSY AND PETER WERE IN THE LIVING ROOM WHEN Falcon got home. They were looking through a shoebox full of photographs to find a recent snapshot of Toody for the police. Neither Missy nor Peter was any good at photography, so most of the pictures either were blurry or cut off the top of Toody's head.

They looked up to see Falcon and smiled at their daughter. She could see that Missy had been crying, and her father's eyes were red, too. Peter gave her a hug.

"We've called out for Mexican from Carlita's," he said. "Don't want to miss any phone calls. Want to come with me to pick it up?" Missy went into the kitchen, saying, "You want milk or grape juice with dinner?"

"Milk, for the hotness," said Falcon, wondering how she was going to get her parents to eat the Slow Food in the morning. She put the carton in her treasure box to keep it safe and grabbed her denim jacket.

Carlita's was just around the corner on Columbus Avenue. It was nice to be walking with Peter in New York, and for a few minutes it felt like it used to, before the divorce, when going around the corner for Mexican, or for sushi at Kendo's, was an ordinary thing to do.

"Penny?" said Peter.

"I was just thinking," said Falcon.

"I know, that's why I'm giving you a penny. For your thoughts." Her father put a coin in her hand.

"That's a quarter."

"Inflation," said Peter. "What's up, little bird? You don't still think it's your fault that Toody's . . . that Toody is missing, do you?"

Falcon knew Peter had started to say, "Toody's dead" and she couldn't stand that. She pulled on her father's arm.

"Daddy, you've got to believe me! It's all true, what I said about dragonsbreath and Blinda, and there's more. Toody's fine, he's with Egg in Australia and he—"

Peter jerked his arm away and grabbed her by the shoulders, speaking in a tense furious voice she had never heard before.

"Falcon, stop it! It's not helping us, it won't help you. You're hurting Missy, you're hurting me when you go on like this. Oh, I know you all had fun with that dragon game, but it's got to stop now. Aunt Emily, she's old and . . . she imagines things, but you have to have more sense. You have to grow up, Falcon."

His words felt like a slap, and she walked on beside him in silence, stiff-legged as a robot, into the warm smell and music of Carlita's.

Carlita herself handed Peter the shopping bag of food and touched his arm, her face full of sorrow.

"*Lo siento*, Señor Davies. I pray for your boy."

Peter muttered something and they walked home. They rode up in the elevator without saying a word.

Outside 4B, Peter took Falcon's hand.

"I'm sorry, bird. I shouldn't have yelled at you, I know you don't mean to . . . look, just hold off on the magic stuff for the time being, okay? Promise?"

Falcon nodded but didn't meet her father's eyes, and they walked in.

Missy had put two beers and a tall glass of milk on the coffee table in the living room and set three places; they all liked sitting on the floor to eat instead of on chairs. Falcon put a paper napkin at each place, wishing she were anywhere but here. The spicy smell of the food made her feel sick.

"Did you get flan, Peter?" asked Missy. "Toody loves—" She stopped and bit her lip. Falcon patted her mother's arm, seeing Toody in her mind, on the beach with Egg, and wishing she could tell her mother that Toody was fine. But she had promised not to talk about magic, and they wouldn't listen anyway, so she just kept on patting.

"I'm sure he's okay," she said. "I sort of . . . dreamed about him and he was fine, he really was." She could feel her father's eyes watching her, like a warning. The phone rang and they all jumped up. Missy seized it and listened, with Peter and Falcon staring at her as though they could make the caller say what they wanted to hear just by concentrating. It was maddening to hear only one end of the conversation.

"He *is?*" said Missy. "But it seems so . . ."

"Gurblegurblegurble," said the phone.

"Not at all? Then you think that maybe my son . . . ? Really?"

"Gurblegurble."

"Oh, thank you, Lieutenant, that's so encouraging." She hung up, shaking her head.

"Lieutenant Eddler says they found Mr. Bender and he's going to be fine."

"What?!" cried Peter and Falcon together.

"Yes, it's the weirdest thing. A rancher in Wyoming found this round yellow flat thing in his cow pasture. It was covering a three-hundred-foot circle of grass, so he tried to move it but it was too big. He rolled it up tight, and when he did, it spoke. It said, 'I'll sue!' Well, he was pretty surprised, but he took it home and called the sheriff. There was a lot of fuss and medical examinations and all, but anyhow it turned out to be Mr. Bender. Now he's in a hospital in Los Angeles and they say he's going to be fine, eventually. He's suing the airline, the manufacturer of the plane, his travel agent, the rancher, the sheriff, the hospital, and his wife for not making more of an effort to find him."

Peter's face turned bright red and he snatched up the phone.

"Missy, that's just . . . ridiculous, it's impossible! Why didn't you let me talk to Eddler—I'm sure you got it wrong." He dialed but the line was busy and he crashed the phone down, running his hands through his hair in frustration. Missy stood scowling at him with her hands on her hips.

"Excuse *me*, Peter Davies, but do you really think I'm too stupid to understand what Lieutenant Eddler was saying? Maybe there are some things in the world that you don't understand, maybe you don't know everything."

Peter took a few deep breaths, and Falcon knew he was counting to ten to keep from losing his temper. She held her breath, sitting perfectly still as her father's face returned to its normal color.

"I . . . I'm sorry, Miss," he said. "The whole thing is so terribly odd, and I just hate to think of Toody . . ." He gulped, and both of Falcon's parents were quiet for a minute, looking sick at the thought of Toody all flattened. Then Peter pointed out that as Toody weighed only forty-three pounds he would not fall nearly so heavily as big Mr. Bender. This made them so much more hopeful about Toody that they were quite cheerful over dinner. But Falcon just pushed her food around. The truth she couldn't talk about filled her up as though she had eaten too much, and she could hardly swallow. She ate a shrimp and drank a little milk.

"How about some ice cream to cool off your mouth,

bird?" Peter was opening a carton of raspberry ripple from Gabriel's Café.

"No thanks, I'm really tired," she said and went to her room.

When Missy came to tuck Falcon in, she sat on the bed beside her and took her hand.

"You're right not to give up, Falcon. We'll keep on looking and hoping, shall we?"

Falcon nodded and Missy gave her a good-night hug. "Thank you, little bird," she said and left the room. After a few minutes the door creaked open.

"Falcon?" said her father's voice in a whisper. "Are you awake?" Falcon shut her eyes tight and concentrated on breathing slowly and evenly like someone in a deep sleep.

"I told you she was asleep, Peter; she's exhausted," said Missy. "You can talk to her tomorrow." The door closed but Falcon could still hear her parents' voices.

"I tell you, Missy, there's something fishy about this whole thing—that story about floating down out of the sky, all that stuff about dragons and witches, and you and Emily encouraging her, and now this Mr. Bender . . . well, I just don't believe it, that's all!"

"Why are you so . . . ? You work with shamans, for heaven's sake—they believe in magic and you respect *them*. Why can't you believe your own daughter?"

"That's different. You know perfectly well it's not their magic I believe in, it's the power of the belief itself, and—"

"Oh, Peter, will you just please *hush!* And anyhow it was just one dragon, and I saw it, too!" Falcon heard a strangled sob. "And she was beautiful!" A door slammed.

Falcon opened her eyes and lay there looking at the night sky through her window, her knees drawn up to her chest.

"I'm not going to cry," she said aloud. Henry walked up from his place at the foot of the bed and sprawled out on the pillow facing her, his yellow eyes four inches from her own.

"I wish you could talk like Augustus," she said. Henry just purred and kneaded her arm gently with his furry paws till she fell asleep.

CHAPTER
SEVEN

I N THE MORNING FALCON GOT UP BEFORE FIVE AND sneaked into the kitchen with the box of Slow Food. She opened it and looked inside. It looked and smelled exactly like cornflakes, and she thought about tasting it but decided she'd better not. As quietly as possible she took the half-full box of cornflakes from the cupboard, poured in the Slow Food, closed the box, and tiptoed back to bed.

She woke again at six-thirty to hear her parents talking in the kitchen. She listened for a minute. They didn't sound mad. They hardly ever stayed mad overnight anymore; that was one good thing about the divorce. Missy, she knew, would be half asleep, wearing a ratty old bathrobe with her hair every which way, while Peter would be showered and dressed and full of beans. She got up, went into the kitchen, and sat down, trying not to stare at the box of cornflakes.

"Hey, birdlet," said her father. "Toast or cereal? Or both?"

"Toast. I'll make it," she said, putting two slices of raisin bread into the toaster and pressing the lever. Behind her she heard the rustling sound of cereal being poured into two bowls. She couldn't bear to watch, so she stared and stared at the hot orange wires inside the toaster, smelling the scent of scorching raisins. What if just Peter ate the Slow Food? Missy sometimes didn't have breakfast till noon. And what would the Slow Food do anyhow? What if it didn't work, as Blinda Cholmondely's spells often didn't, according to Aunt Emily? She listened carefully and was pretty sure she heard two people crunching cornflakes. The toast popped up and she buttered it, put it on a plate, and turned around. Her parents were eating cornflakes, Missy with her head propped on one hand and her eyes half shut.

Falcon sat down and squeezed honey onto her toast from the plastic bear, feeling both disappointed and relieved. She would have to leave for Aunt Emily's soon, and how would she explain that to her parents? She glanced at the kitchen clock and was surprised to see it had stopped at six forty-seven. That was odd, as it was an electric clock and there was obviously no power failure— the toaster was working and the lights were still on. She looked at her parents.

Missy's spoon had stopped halfway to her mouth and Peter's was frozen in the act of dipping it into his bowl for another bite. His mouth was open and he had the look on his face he always got when he was about to say something funny. Falcon waited for them to move. Nothing happened. She noticed that it was unusually quiet, even though the window that faced 77th Street was wide open. She looked out and saw that traffic had stopped, for no reason that she could see, and that Eddie, the morning doorman, was standing outside number 16 reaching out to pet Mrs. Haiken's airedale. The dog stood on its hind legs with its mouth open and Mrs. Haiken's mouth was open, too, as though she were about to speak. Nobody and nothing moved, and Falcon saw to her amazement that three pigeons were poised in the air several feet above the sidewalk. As far as she could see, she was the only thing moving on the Upper West Side.

"Slow Food!" she said out loud, and turned away from the window. Her parents were still frozen in mid-mouthful, and several white drops of milk from Missy's spoon hung suspended just above her bowl.

Falcon decided to leave a note just in case the Slow Food wore off before she got back from Australia. She took a page from her French notebook and wrote:

Dear Missy & Peter,

I have gone to find Toody in Australia. I know he is there but I can't tell you how I know because I promised. He is not flat, he is fine. Aunt Emily is helping and she will explain, except you won't believe her because you are grownups. I'll be back soon.

Love, Falcon

She put the note on the table under the sugar bowl, which to her surprise had become much heavier than usual. Then she let herself out of the apartment and headed for the elevator. After a few seconds of pushing the button, she realized that, like everything else, it was stuck. She ran down the stairs and stepped out onto West 77th Street through the lobby door, which was open, fortunately. She looked at a taxicab stopped across the street, the driver holding a half-eaten bagel in mid-bite. She would have to walk across the park to get to Aunt Emily's and she would have to hurry. Her watch, which was still working, said 7:02. Well, at least there wouldn't be any traffic to slow her down. She jogged up Central Park West to 81st Street and walked across on the 79th Street transverse, passing a stopped number 79 bus and a lot of cars on the way. Then down Fifth Avenue to 66th Street and over to number 12. It took all her strength to open the lobby door. She squeezed past Aunt Emily's doorman and paused to catch her breath before running up the three flights of stairs to the roof, where she emerged gasping. There was Aunt Emily, leaning on her cane next to an enormous, scaly, gray-green dragon with tattered leathery wings and a sleepy expression. It was 7:59 A.M.

"Ah, Falcon, my dear. Good morning! Would you like some orange juice?" Aunt Emily handed her a carton of cold juice, which Falcon gulped thirstily, watching the dragon, who stared back with half-closed ruby eyes.

"Now then," said Aunt Emily, "Dirus, this is Emily

Falcon Davies. Falcon, this is Dirus Horribilus, the Scourge of Babylon."

The dragon shuffled forward, its wings rattling like the ribs of an old umbrella, and extended its right claw to Falcon, who recoiled, not wanting to be scorched. Aunt Emily said, "It's all right, dear, Dirus is one of the Old Ones, he has little fire left except for his burning heart. He will not harm you."

Falcon took one of the dragon's talons in her hand. It was rough and dry to the touch and only slightly warm. Dirus spoke in a language that Falcon didn't understand, his voice deep and echoing like that of someone shouting in a cave.

"What did he say?" she asked.

"He says, 'I will become young in deeds in spite of my years. I shall carry out the task assigned me.' It's a misquote from Euripides."

"But what does it mean?"

"Just what he says. He's going to take you to the Arafura Sea to find Toody."

Falcon stared at the ancient dragon, who was more than twice the size of an elephant. He was gray-green all over like old bronze, except for his bright crimson eyes and a faint orange glow in his chest. His breath came in white puffs from his nostrils and his ragged wings were forty feet wide from tip to tip. *Dirus Horribilus,* she thought and took a deep breath. The dragon extended one enormous hind leg like a ballet dancer and motioned toward it with his head. Falcon put one cautious foot onto the broad scaly surface, and finding it steady under her, she climbed up the leg to his crested back.

"Just behind the wing, dear, that's the way," said Aunt Emily, handing her a paper bag of sandwiches and craning her neck to look up at her great-great-niece. Falcon found that she could sit astride Dirus's back between two crests, the one behind her like the back of a chair and the one in front for holding on. Dirus stretched his wings out to their full width and shuffled forward a few steps.

"Wait!" said Falcon. "How will we talk if he only speaks ancient Greek?"

"Don't worry; he's picked up a good deal of English in the last thousand years. After all, he was around when it was invented, you know. Oh, and don't worry if he falls asleep now and then; he's very old."

"But . . ." Falcon began, but it was too late. Dirus was trotting toward the edge of the roof with surprising speed, and in a moment they were airborne.

"Goodbye! Goodbye!" called Aunt Emily, waving her cane as they circled higher and higher into the pale blue sky of an April morning.

CHAPTER EIGHT

Looking down, Falcon saw the city was still frozen, all traffic stopped, a little girl jumping rope floating inches above the sidewalk, and a squirrel in mid-leap hanging suspended from a tree limb. The white steam that boils up from the bowels of the city stood solid as marble columns, and the water from the Grand Army Plaza fountain hung like a crystal chandelier in the still air.

The dragon turned west and they flew over the park and toward the Hudson River. The effects of the Slow Food seemed to stop there, and they passed through a rising cloud of foul brown smoke as they flew over the northeastern edge of New Jersey. Dirus coughed and said something Greekish.

"I don't understand," said Falcon.

"If you're queasy or pale, take courage, don't quail.

We will soon be beyond Jersey's pestilent pond; you'll be fine if you just don't inhale," said the dragon.

"That's awful!" said Falcon.

Dirus rumbled with laughter as the industrial grayness below them gave way to the green patchwork of western New Jersey's farm country.

They continued west over the vast continent, mile after mile clad in the colors of early spring with snow shining white from the still frozen mountaintops. Endless black ribbons of asphalt speckled with brightly colored cars and trucks snaked through the land, spreading out into broad carpets of gray-brown malls and housing developments. Falcon was surprised to see how ugly the towns looked from the sky, and she felt relieved when they reached the Midwest, with its pale green sea of young corn and wheat. The towns here were just as ugly but there weren't so many of them, and she could see rivers and lakes flashing blue amid the green. She knew they still had a long way to go, and she did some stretching exercises, holding on to Dirus's crest with one hand. *If only I hadn't been so tired from sitting,* she thought, *I'd have been paying attention and I could've stopped Toody from opening that door. I should have; he was my responsibility.* He always had been, from the time she was six, when they brought him home from the hospital, round-faced and grinning, as though the world were one huge, hilarious joke.

Even though she hadn't wanted to spend this particular Christmas in Australia, one good thing about being with her father was that she wasn't in charge of Toody all the time. Whenever she and her brother visited Peter, whether in Australia or South America or England, she knew that as soon as she saw him waiting at the arrival gate, she could hand Toody over to him.

She had tried to talk to Peter about the way Missy left Toody in her care all the time, but he just looked uncomfortable and muttered something about not interfering.

"But you're my father, you're supposed to interfere," she said. Peter was assembling a seafood lasagna and didn't answer right away. He put the baking dish into the oven and turned around.

"Look, bird, the only way your mother and I can get along is by not fighting about you and Tood. Don't you remember how it was? You hated it—you know you did." He grinned at her. "Dinner'll be ready in an hour; go have a swim, why don't you?"

Falcon did remember coming home from school and standing outside the door of 4B, hearing the yelling. She remembered lying in bed, straining to make out the words in the murmurs from the next room; the way the sound of slammed doors seemed to go right through her; sitting at the dinner table when every word sounded like an insult. She sighed.

"Hey," said Peter. "It's not so bad, is it, bird? We're all happy now."

She went to the beach, and it was great not having to drag Toody along, but she didn't think her father understood that when you are used to taking care of someone nine months of the year, you can't just turn it off like a faucet.

The Midwest unrolled beneath them in endless waves of grass. Falcon fell asleep over Iowa, lulled by the motion of flight and the soothing warmth of the dragon's body.

In 4B, Missy's spoon clattered into her bowl, splashing milk onto the table.

". . . otter space," said Peter.

"What?" Missy mopped at the milk with her napkin.

"I said, 'Where do otters come from?' It's a joke. Falcon, don't you. . . . Hey, where is she?"

"Oh my god, Peter, look!" Missy handed him the note, soggy with milk. Peter read it and stood up so fast his chair fell over backward.

"Emily!" he said. "That crazy aunt of yours, mixed up in this mess. I might have known."

Missy yelled at Peter and he yelled back the whole time she was getting dressed, and all the way over to Emily's in the cab. They stopped when they got to number 12 East 66th Street, and Missy, her eyes red, asked the doorman to announce them. They rode up in the elevator without speaking.

Emily opened the door and said, "I've been expecting you, my dears. Sit down, won't you?"

"Emily, I will not sit down until you tell me where Falcon is!" Peter shouted, towering over the old lady.

"Well," she said, turning her back on him and lowering herself into a straight-backed armchair, "I shall sit, in any case. I'm too old to discuss things standing up." She waited, and finally Missy and Peter sat down facing her on the edge of the sofa, as far apart as possible.

"Emily," said Missy, clasping her hands in front of her, "please tell us, if you know, where is Falcon?"

Emily looked at her watch, which had extra-large numbers so she could see them without her glasses. "Over Wyoming, I should think," she said. "Or perhaps California, depending on the wind speed."

Peter looked as though he were about to explode, but as Great-Aunt Emily refused to argue or get excited, he and Missy were forced to listen as she told them everything. At last she finished and took a sip of water from the glass by her side.

"That's most of it," she said, patting her lips with a handkerchief. "I know you think I am quite demented, Peter, but Missy, you know I'm telling the truth, don't you, my dear?"

Missy took a deep breath. "Yes, I do. Peter, it's all part of the same thing: Toody, Falcon, Mr. Bender—don't you see? Do you really think that Emily and Falcon and the NYPD and I could all be crazy at once? It's magic, Peter, and it's real, as real as . . ."

"Socks," said Aunt Emily, smiling at her niece.

"Yes," said Missy, taking her great-aunt's hand. "As real as socks."

Peter sat with his head in his hands. At last he looked up.

"Magic," he said. "I just don't know, it seems so . . ." He stood up. "I'm sorry, Emily, I didn't mean to shout."

The old lady reached up and patted his shoulder.

"It's all right, my dear. Now then, there's a flight to Sydney at noon, I believe; you should make it if you leave now. And try not to worry. There's more to that girl of yours than you know, and more things in heaven and earth than are dreamt of in your philosophy, as Mr. Shakespeare says."

When Falcon awoke from her nap, they were flying over what she thought of as the square states: Colorado, Wyoming, Utah. When she was little she had had a jigsaw puzzle map of the United States. You could fit Wyoming into the Colorado space and vice versa, so she never could remember where was which. Now, in April, the land looked greener and prettier than she remembered from her last flight, in December, when it was all dull, dead brown patched with snow.

She took the paper bag out of her pocket and ate a sandwich, leaning back against the curve of Dirus's back. *This is a really neat way to travel,* she thought, *much more comfortable than any airplane seat.* She wished Aunt Emily had packed an orange or some juice.

"Drinky poo?" asked the dragon, turning his head to stare at her with sleepy red eyes.

"Uh, yes please," said Falcon, wondering where the "drinky poo" would come from.

Dirus veered toward a cloud bank and passed the tip of his right wing through it as though he were slicing an angel food cake. A stream of rainwater trickled along his wing and as he tipped it up Falcon was able to get a good drink by leaning to one side and putting her mouth in its path. It was rather messy and the ends of her hair got wet, but it quenched her thirst perfectly well. They were over the Pacific now, and too high to see anything but blue-green water that seemed to go on forever. Falcon knew from her trips to see Peter that this would be the longest leg of the voyage, though they seemed to be making very good time. Her watch said eleven o'clock and she tried to figure out when they would land in Australia going at this rate, but the time zones were too confusing.

She wondered if the Slow Food had worn off yet, and whether Missy and Peter had read her note. She began to pick at a hangnail on the side of her thumb. Had she added to her parents' worry about Toody by leaving? Should she have tried to explain again about Blinda Cholmondely and Egg, in spite of her promise? She knew they wouldn't have believed her.

Falcon heard sea gulls calling and looked down to see that they were nearing land. Dirus flew lower and she smelled pine and eucalyptus. They passed over dense forest and banked toward the distant sparkle of blue water.

"Your brother lies over the ocean. Your brother lies over the sea. So fasten your seatbelt, dear Falcon. I'll bet that you're dying to pee!" sang Dirus in his echoey voice.

Falcon hadn't thought of it till the dragon mentioned it, but now she really had to go. Between Dirus's awful poetry and her full bladder, she would be very glad when this part of her journey was over.

They flew in descending circles and landed at last on a strip of beach that looked quite familiar. It was the same beach she had seen on Blinda's television, and sure enough, there on the shore were Toody and Egg. Toody was jumping up and down and yelling, and as soon as Dirus landed he ran toward them.

"YAY! FALCON!" he shouted as his sister climbed down and hugged him. "Where's Missy?" he said.

"She's still in New York and so's Peter. They're looking for you." Toody's face turned red and he got ready to roar.

"Why are they looking for me there, I'm here! Why didn't you bring them? Why—"

"I am!" said Falcon. "I mean I'm taking you back, as soon as I go to the bathroom." She ran into the bushes and came back feeling much better and ready to go home. "Come on," she said to her brother. She turned to Dirus, but the huge beast had curled up on the hot sand and fallen fast asleep. No amount of shouting or shaking would wake him. Just when she had decided to give him a good kick, Egg, who had not spoken till now, said, "A stirring dwarf we do allowance give before a sleeping dragon."

Falcon put her foot down and looked at Egg. On Blinda's TV the dragon had looked pretty much like the one she had last seen soaring into the night over New

York City, only bigger. She wished she could put on a pair of oven mitts and hug her the way she used to. But now she saw that Egg was not only bigger and thinner, she was much hotter. She was actually on fire; tiny flames fringed the edges of her wings and crest, and Falcon remembered hearing about Aunt Emily's friend St. George, whose hair and eyebrows were frizzed by dragonfire and whose face was permanently sunburned from dancing with dragons. She stepped back and gazed up at Egg, seeing twin Falcons reflected in the dragon's clear turquoise eyes, and for the moment at least, her worries vanished. When she looked into that deep cool blue, she knew she was strong enough and smart enough to do whatever she needed to do, and it didn't seem so important that they get back immediately, or that Dirus wouldn't wake up, or that Missy and Peter might be angry with her for leaving. She smiled and said, "You've gotten so big and hot!"

Egg did not reply but turned to Toody, who was unwrapping a cheese sandwich from Falcon's paper bag. The little boy set the sandwich down on the sand and the dragon blew gently on it. It was instantly toasted to a perfect golden brown with the cheese all gooey inside.

"Thanks, Egg," said Toody, and he took a cautious bite. "Good," he mumbled around a mouthful of melted cheese. Falcon stared at her little brother. She would never have thought to ask Egg to make a grilled cheese sandwich. It was so practical. She sat down beside him. Maybe it would be all right to spend the night here. Surely Dirus would be awake by morning and they could fly back then.

She supposed a flight of nine thousand miles must be tiring for an old dragon.

She felt Egg's heat on her face as the dragon stood nearby. *She's not cute anymore,* thought Falcon, remembering Egg's round rubbery tummy and baby squeaks. She had changed, and now there was beauty and power in the arch of her long neck and the angle of her wings. She had become one of the shining magical beings Aunt Emily had talked about. "When magic comes, it comes for a reason," Aunt Emily had said. Had Egg come back to save her life, and Toody's? She had given Egg her freedom; was this her reward?

"I wish Peter could see you," she said. "You are so beautiful and so real."

Before Egg could speak, Toody, who had finished his sandwich, tugged at Falcon's sleeve.

"I want to go home now, Falcon."

"We can't go yet, Tood, we have to wait till Dirus wakes up." The little boy's lip trembled.

"Wake him up now—I want to go!"

"Sprinkle cool patience on thy distemper, Tudor, and let sleep shut up sorrow's eye," said Egg.

"*You* shut up," said Toody, and he stomped off toward the woods.

"Hey!" said Falcon. "Where are you going?"

"To my house," he said over his shoulder. Falcon followed, leaving the two dragons on the beach while Toody led the way along a narrow path that wound through the trees till they came to a small grassy clearing. To Falcon's amazement, there stood a small hut made of leaves and branches. It was only a hut, but it looked sturdy and much neater than anything her kid brother could possibly have built. Toody pulled aside the screen of woven grasses that concealed the doorway and stepped inside. His sister followed behind him. The late afternoon sun poured in through the entrance, and Falcon could see that the hut was empty except for two sleeping bags decorated with Disney characters.

"Where'd you get those?" she asked, staring. "How did you build this hut?"

"It's my house, the People helped me," said Toody, rummaging inside a sleeping bag and pulling out a plastic bag with the name "Woolworths" printed on it. "Harry'll wake up that old dragon, you'll see." He reached inside the bag and handed Falcon a new red toothbrush still in its box.

"They brought this for you, they said you'd come."

"They who? What people, what do you mean? And who's Harry?"

"They look like Peter's friends," said Toody. "They said Egg was a Spirit Bean. She cut the branches for my house, see?"

The little boy pointed at the poles that supported the roof, and Falcon saw they were blackened at the bottom as though they had been cut not with steel but with fire.

Toody pulled a can of baked beans from under one of

the sleeping bags. "You can have this for supper. There's no more samwiches. And there's some pawpaw. You can have the Mickey bag."

It is annoying to be told what to do by your kid brother, and for a moment Falcon was going to refuse the beans, but she was hungry. She took the plastic spoon Toody gave her, popped the lid off the can, and began to eat. Toody watched her with a pleased expression. He stuck out his belly, clasped his hands behind his back, and marched up and down the hut.

"I am your good gracious host," he said, strutting. Falcon couldn't help laughing, he was so ridiculous. Then she remembered Dirus, sound asleep on the beach. Would he wake up in the morning? How long would a thousand-year-old dragon sleep, anyhow?

Her brother picked up a toothbrush and a tube of paste. "Come on," he said. "We have to brush." Falcon followed him through the clearing to a spring that bubbled up between the roots of an enormous eucalyptus tree. The children brushed their teeth and took a good drink of the cool water before returning to the hut. Toody climbed into his sleeping bag and so did Falcon, though she was sure she'd never get to sleep with all the things she had to worry about jangling around in her brain.

It was surprising how well her little brother had gotten along without her. She remembered how good he was with Lego and wondered how much work he had actually done on this quite comfortable hut. Now he brushed his teeth without being told and he had made all these friends, whoever they were. *Of course he's just a baby,* she thought. *He needs a lot of help, and he's just not serious like me. He never seems to worry about anything,* she thought, lying there and listening to the wind in the trees.

"'Night, Falcon," said her brother.

"'Night, Tood," she said. *No, he never has any problems, he just clowns his way through life, singing and making jokes, no responsibilities, just jokes and beans, jokes and beans . . .*

CHAPTER NINE

FALCON OPENED HER EYES AND SCREAMED. A WRINKLED black face hung in the air two inches from her own, staring at her with huge dark eyes.

"Blimey! Din't mean to scare ye, bird-girl," said the face as it pulled away. Falcon struggled to sit up, realized where she was, and pulled down the zipper of her sleeping bag. Toody ran into the hut carrying a long fork with a piece of bread on it.

"Why are you yelling at Harry? He's my friend."

Falcon looked at the old man, who was now squatting in a corner of the hut, watching her with lively brown eyes.

"You sleep rough, girlie," he said. "Too many voices in your head, I reckon."

"I wasn't asleep!" said Falcon. "I was . . . thinking, with my eyes closed."

"You were so!" said Toody. "I've been up for hours, we made breakfast. Come on!"

Falcon stepped out into bright sunlight to the delicious smells of frying bacon and toast. A skillet was balanced on two stones over a small fire, and it held a pile of fried bacon that was pushed over to one side to make room for eggs sizzling in the hot fat. Toody crouched by the hearth toasting a thick slice of bread over the flame. A tin plate piled high with toast sat nearby, next to a jar of marmalade, a pot of tea, and a small can of condensed milk.

"She makes a jolly good fire for a Yankee dragon, young lady; a right blazer. Here, drink up." The old man handed Falcon a mug. The tea was sweet and almost too hot to drink.

"I made the toast," said Toody, taking a plate of eggs, bacon, toast, and marmalade carefully in both hands and handing it to Falcon. Some of the toast was scorched, but Falcon ate it all and wiped up the last of the egg with a crust. She sat sipping tea and watching Harry as he cleaned the breakfast things with sand and water from the spring and packed them neatly into his knapsack.

"Did he build your house?" she whispered to her brother. He shook his head, stuffing the last piece of toast and marmalade into his mouth whole. He chewed, swallowed with some difficulty, and shook his head again, wiping his sticky face with the back of his hand.

"The others did and I helped. Harry comes to talk with Egg and to sing. Falcon, is Missy coming today?"

"Missy? No, she doesn't even know where we are; how could she come? We have to go, we have to wake up Dirus and go home." She stood up and took his hand and they headed for the beach, with Harry trailing after them, chanting to himself. The huge gray-green mound that was Dirus snored gently next to Egg, who stood watch, the flames along her wings flickering in the breeze. The sand under her had melted into a puddle of molten glass.

"Dirus!" called Falcon. "Dirus, wake UP!" Toody joined in and both children shouted until they were hoarse, but it was no use. The old dragon slept on, his scaly hide rippling now and then with some dream of ancient times and long-ago dances. Harry hunkered down on the sand, laughing till tears came to his eyes.

"No use shouting," he said, when he could speak. "That old dragon, he'll kip till he wakes."

"But how will we get home? We're in the middle of nowhere!" said Falcon.

"Everywhere's somewhere, Toody's old sister. This is Arnhem Land and it's home to the People and that's me."

"I'm sorry," said Falcon. "I didn't mean . . ."

Harry ignored her and stared up at the sky. Toody copied him, squatting with his elbows resting on his knees and his head thrown back. Falcon looked up. The sky arched above them, vastly blue with a few small wispy clouds in the distance.

"What are we looking at?" she asked.

The old man did not answer. Far away over the sea three gulls circled, looking for fish. A bright yellow bird, much larger than the others, flew into their midst, shattering their smooth circles and sending them squawking off in different directions. The ungainly interloper flapped across the water nearer and nearer to the watchers on the beach. *That's a huge bird,* thought Falcon. *Poor thing, it seems to be injured, it's so clumsy, it's . . . BLINDA!* She was on her feet running along the edge of the surf as the witch, dressed in an enormous yellow raincoat, hiking boots, and a wide-brimmed straw hat, zigzagged over the waves astride her shooting stick to land with a bump on the shore. The shooting stick collapsed on impact, dumping her onto the sand. She took Falcon's outstretched hand and stood up, brushing herself off and straightening her clothes.

"Whoosha!" she said. "Wotta ride!" She smiled happily at Falcon, Toody, and Harry, who bowed deeply. Toody copied him.

"This is Blinda Cholmondely, pronounced Chumley," said Falcon. "Blinda, this is—"

"Oh, I know!" said Blinda, bending down to see into the faces of Harry and Toody, who were still bowing. Unfortunately, just at that moment they straightened up and Harry's head collided with Blinda's with a loud crack. "OW!" they said.

"Very honored to meet you, ma'am, I'm sure," said Harry, rubbing his skull and blinking rapidly to clear his vision.

"Me too, me too," said the witch, looking dazed.

"What are you doing here?" asked Falcon. Blinda was examining herself in a small mirror she had pulled out of the pocket of her raincoat. Satisfied that there was no permanent damage from her encounter with Harry's head, she put it away.

"I'm here to help you two get home, of course. Emily and I saw you on TV; I told her Dirus would never be able to fly both ways without a nap. Now look at him!"

They all stared at the enormous pile of gray-green dragon sleeping on the beach some distance away. Egg still stood watch nearby, the flames that outlined her scarlet body almost invisible in the bright sunlight. All you could see was the shimmer of hot air, like waves of heat rising from a summer sidewalk. The young dragon was fidgeting, shifting from one foot to the other, and making a low, anxious sound. Falcon walked over and looked up at her.

"Can you help, Egg? Without hurting him, I mean?"

"Dragonfire can't hurt a dragon," said Blinda, coming up behind her. "And it would take a lot of courage for Egg to disturb Dirus. . . . He's a legend, you know."

"But maybe she could wake him up," said Falcon.

They stood watching Dirus for several minutes. Suddenly Egg thrust her long neck forward and roared into the old dragon's ear, sending out a great blast of fire and smoke and scaring them all very much.

When the smoke cleared, Dirus was sleeping as soundly as ever. He curled one foot over his nose, muttering, "Just ten more years, Ma," and began to snore.

Egg walked off a few steps and turned her back. Falcon started toward her, but a blushing dragon is 4.7

times hotter than normal and Falcon couldn't get near her. She went back to Dirus and the others.

"He's been asleep for more than twelve hours," said Falcon. "Don't you think he'll wake up soon?"

"Twelve hours!" said Blinda. "That's nothing to a dragon. Twelve years it could be, or twelve hundred. Look at Vesuvius." Falcon looked puzzled.

"Vesuvius," said the witch. "You know, Krakatoa, Hibok-Hibok, Mount St. Helen's? Honestly, don't they teach anything in these schools? Volcanoes!"

"I know about volcanoes," said Falcon, "but I don't see—"

"Well, what do you think volcanoes are, for heaven's sake! They're dragon lairs, where dragons go to sleep for years and years sometimes. And then of course when they wake up, there's an awful ruckus. Dragons always wake up grumpy, even the nice ones. Why, it was a cousin of Dirus's who destroyed Pompeii in seventy-nine. Didn't mean to, of course, but there you are."

Falcon, who had studied volcanoes in school, found all this very hard to believe, but she thought it might not be a good idea to argue about it just now.

"Can you help us get home then, Blinda?" Falcon looked at the collapsed shooting stick, which didn't look like it could hold three people.

"Not on that stupid thing," said Blinda, giving it a kick. "Don't know what I was thinking, it's most unreliable. You can't beat a good old-fashioned broomstick, when all's said and done."

"We got plenty o' broomsticks, ma'am," said Harry respectfully. "Honored to give you our very best, all you need."

Blinda beamed at him and struggled out of the raincoat, which was much too big for her (it belonged to Aunt Emily, who was a good deal taller). Underneath it she wore a rather astonishing jump suit made of green-and-white-checked gingham with many pockets. She had designed it herself. "Woof!" she said. "That's better. It's hot here, isn't it? Now where was I? Oh yes, broomsticks. Thank you very much, dear, but it wouldn't work, I'm afraid. Couldn't get three on any broomstick, and Falcon and Toody here, well." She leaned over and whispered to Harry behind her hand. "They're not witches, you see. Not their fault, born that way. Human beings."

Falcon started to protest till Harry grinned at her and shook his head behind Blinda's back. The witch was pulling various things out of the capacious pockets of her jump suit.

Falcon, Toody, and Harry watched as she laid the objects out on the sand. A sugar lump, a small brown bean, a toy cow made of plastic, a refrigerator magnet in the shape of a coffeepot, and a silver thimble. The witch nodded with satisfaction, scooped all the objects into her hat, and set off toward the two dragons with Falcon, Toody, and Harry hurrying along behind. Blinda, though plump, was a fast walker.

"You can call dragons from their fast asleep and so can

I and so can anyone, but will they come when you do call for them?" asked Egg, watching Blinda. The witch did not reply. Keeping a respectful distance from the young dragon, she dug a hole in the sand near Dirus's sleeping head. She put the coffeepot magnet in the middle with the bean, the sugar lump, and the cow beside it. Then she filled the thimble with seawater, set it carefully in the hole, and stood back. "Ready?" she asked.

"All things are ready if our minds be so," said Egg, and she rose on the tips of her talons to get a better angle. Blinda stood and pointed at the hole. "Coffea arabica, Robusta insomnia, eye of Argus, argybargus, lava, kava, java JUMP!" As she spoke, Egg snorted a stream of fire into the hole in the sand, which instantly bubbled up into a flaming brown and silver mass that gave off a delicious and familiar smell. When the flames died down, in place of the hole there stood a large silver bucket filled to the brim with creamy, foamy, fragrant liquid. The sandy hole had turned to glass.

"Cappuccino!" said Toody. "Can I have some? Is it decaf?"

"Most definitely *not*," said Blinda. The hot strong coffee, mixed with steamed milk and sugar, sent its seductive aroma into the air and into the nostrils of the sleeping dragon. The great creature stirred, opened one crimson eye, and inhaled deeply. His other eye opened and he yawned a most monstrous yawn, so that they could see his long blue tongue and the rows of foot-long teeth that lined his terrible jaws. Two of the teeth had gold fillings in them and Falcon wondered what sort of creature would be a dentist to dragons.

"No cinnamon?" said Dirus. He took a long drink of the cappuccino, getting foam all over his nose. "Dee-lishus!" he said, and finished it off. To Falcon and Toody's surprise, the silver bucket filled up again with a loud gurgle, the way a toilet does when you flush. Harry was not surprised because he was a shaman and expected remarkable things to happen, the world so full of wonders as it is.

Dirus drank forty-seven bucketfuls of cappuccino before he was through, all the while munching on the croissants Blinda provided from her jump-suit pocket, which, like the silver bucket, was never empty.

"Stand back," said the dragon, and the three humans and Blinda moved to a safe distance as Dirus stretched, belched out a coffee-scented burp, and stood up. He spread his wings out to their full length and gave them a shake to settle the scales.

"When time and travel make you low, there's nothing like a cup of Joe," he said. Falcon privately thought Dirus was just about the worst poet she had ever heard, but she knew that nobody can keep people from writing bad poetry.

"Well, all aboard," said Dirus, "if you're ready." He stretched his foreleg out to make a ramp. Toody hugged Harry, who helped him climb onto the dragon's back with

Blinda. They settled themselves comfortably behind his head, but Falcon lingered, looking at Egg shimmering with heat in the sunshine. Were they even now, and was this the end of magic?

She moved as close to the dragon as she could, her eyes narrowing as the heat surrounded her so that she felt her eyebrows curling up like St. George's.

"Egg," she said. "They want to forget you, Missy and Ardene. And Peter." She stopped for a moment, remembering the anger in her father's eyes. "Peter doesn't believe in you at all."

The dragon turned her eyes on Falcon, and as always their cool blue depths calmed her.

"But let thy dauntless mind still fly in triumph over all mistrust," said Egg. "Let proof speak."

Of course! thought Falcon. *Peter lives here!*

"Egg, Peter comes to Arnhem Land all the time. Could I bring him to see you the next time I come to Australia?"

The dragon sighed and sat in a puddle, which instantly vanished with a hiss of steam.

"Truth can never be confirmed enough," she said, "else doubts may never sleep."

Falcon would have liked to stay longer, but Toody was chanting, "Going home, going home, home, home, going HOME!" She climbed up Dirus's leg and sat behind her brother.

"Ta rah! Goodbye, Toody-boy, and you, bird-girl, ta rah!" called Harry, waving as Dirus spread his wings and began to run heavily along the edge of the waves, where the sand was packed hard and smooth. He took off and flew toward Egg so he could take advantage of the thermal created by the young dragon's heat.

"Goodbye, goodbye!" cried Falcon and Toody, waving back. They rose quickly into the air and were soon high over the sea, leaving Egg and Harry far behind, a scarlet shimmer and a small brown shape by the water's edge.

They didn't see the Jeep come hurtling over the sand to pull up beside Harry, nor the tall man who leapt out to stand shouting and waving frantically up at the sky. At last he stopped and seemed really to see Egg for the first time. A look of astonished delight spread over his face as the heat of her flaming hide warmed his face.

"So. It was all true," said Peter.

CHAPTER
TEN

J UST AS ON FALCON'S PREVIOUS FLIGHT, THE JOURNEY OVER
the sea was long and boring, and all three of them fell
asleep. Dirus of course did not, as he had swallowed an
enormous quantity of coffee and would probably be
awake for months. In fact, he had had far too much caf-
feine, even for a dragon, and it had made him jittery. He
was too distracted to notice the multicolored cloud loom-
ing up on his port side, and before he could turn away, he
had flown right into it.

The three sleepers awoke with a start to the smell of
caramel and the sound of bagpipes playing "Loch
Lomond" as they tumbled through a rainbow fog while
still seated on Dirus's back.

"What's happening?" screamed Falcon, holding on to
the dragon with one hand and Toody with the other,
trying to make herself heard over the skirl of bagpipes.

"Ssss-ppp-aaaaccce rrrifftttt," stuttered Dirus, who was struggling to stay right side up as they fell.

"Oh, drat and *double* drat!" said Blinda, whose raincoat had blown up over her head and enveloped her in its yellow folds. Her head poked out and looked down.

"Just relax, Dirus," she said. "No danger, just a slight detour. Didn't you see the rift?"

"Nnnnot exactly," said the old dragon.

"What is it?" asked Toody, who was most interested in the sweet smell that surrounded them. He loved caramel.

"Space rift," said the witch. "It will take us to a parallel universe."

"You mean another planet?" asked Falcon.

"No, it'll still be Earth, only—"

Just at that moment, in a swirl of multicolored mist, they landed gently in a field dotted with wildflowers. A red-headed man in a plaid kilt was sitting nearby eating something out of a paper bag. His bagpipes lay beside him and his nose was pink with sunburn. He looked up.

"Toffee?" he said. Toody scrambled down from the dragon's back and fished a piece of candy from the bag.

"Thanks," he mumbled with his mouth full.

The Scotsman, if that's what he was, stood up as Falcon and Blinda approached with the dragon lumbering behind them. He picked up the bagpipes and bowed low.

"The MacBean of the clan MacBean, at your service," he said.

"Blinda Cholmondely, pronounced Chumley," said

Blinda, "licensed witch, fully accredited, charter member of HOCAS*, all mod cons. And this is Falcon Davies and Dirus Horribilus. You've met Toody." She bowed and The MacBean bowed. So did Falcon, and Dirus placed his right foretalon on his chest and bent stiffly, with a loud creaking of his ancient bones. Toody took another toffee.

The MacBean didn't seem at all surprised by their arrival, nor by the presence of an extremely large dragon, but when Blinda told him about the space rift and parallel universes and needing to get home to New York City, he looked confused and scratched his head with a sticky hand.

"Hoots!" he said. "Well, I don't know about such things as that raft of caramel universals, but as for New York, you're here noo, lass. This is Riverside Park and the city's right there." He pointed to the buildings at the foot of the low hill where they stood. Falcon recognized the upside-down lily shape of the Chrysler Building far to her right, and the spires of St. John the Divine on her left, but most of the other buildings were gone. And everything looked much cleaner and smaller. There seemed to be many more parks; in fact, Central Park seemed to have put out fingers of green that stretched all through the city. She thought they must be around West 79th Street because she could see clear across to the familiar red stone pile of the American Museum of Natural History. There were no tall buildings to block her view, and instead of

* HOCAS: Honorable Order of Conjurers and Sorcerers

being bordered by streets on all sides, the museum was surrounded by parkland dotted here and there with houses and other small buildings. Falcon squinched up her eyes to see more clearly. There were no cars anywhere. Bicycles, tricycles, and pedestrians moved along narrow roads that wove through trees and meadows, while brightly colored trolleys trundled on tracks, stopping now and then to pick up or discharge passengers.

"There's the museem," said Toody, jumping up and down. "We're almost home, let's GO! I wanna see Missy!" He began tugging on Falcon's arm. She looked at her little brother's excited face. How could she tell him they weren't home at all, and that there would be no Missy to greet them?

"Tood, we're not—" she began, when Blinda interrupted.

"Yes, let's go," she said. "Toody, Missy's out so we're going to go find her." Toody stared at the witch. He wanted his mother and he knew his apartment was down there across from the museum. But this pink-cheeked lady in the jump suit was pretty nice.

"Missy's out?" he said.

"Yes," said Blinda. "She's gone to—"

"To shopping?" he said.

"Yes," said Blinda. "She's gone shopping."

Falcon didn't think Blinda should be lying to Toody, but she knew he'd howl if they told him Missy wasn't here so she didn't say anything. Yet what if there were a parallel Missy and parallel Toody and parallel Falcon instead of none at all? Wouldn't that be even more horrible?

The MacBean led them down the hill past a small lake and a brick cottage with a sign over the door that said NESS CAFÉ.

"My own place," said the MacBean. "The wee Loch Ness is mine as well; it keeps me from being homesick for Scotland. Now then, I'll take you to see the mayor, she'll know about your spice rack and parachute unicorns and such."

"I'll meet you at the mayor's place, avoiding further rifts in space," said Dirus. He made a running start down the hill and took off toward the east side, flying low so as not to run into any more space rifts. People glanced up and pointed at him as he passed over their heads; children jumped up and down with excitement to see such a large and handsome dragon.

CHAPTER
ELEVEN

FALCON, TOODY, BLINDA, AND THE MACBEAN WALKED down to the nearest corner and boarded a bright lavender trolley marked HITHER AND YON. There was no fare box, but when they got on, the driver said, "Travel for a song. What'll it be, dearios?" The MacBean cleared his throat and sang four stanzas of "The Bonnets of Bonnie Dundee" in a husky tenor. The driver beamed. "Now that's worth hearing," he said. "You'd not believe some of the caterwauling I have to put up with. Four stanzas, four fares, whither bound?"

"To the mayor's, if ye please, and thank ye kindly," said the MacBean. He and the driver spent the journey singing folksongs while the trolley clickety-clacked across town through Central Park. The park, though it was much bigger, didn't look all that different, but there weren't nearly as many people as Falcon was used to, and no one was hurrying. Most people rode large tricycles or walked and it was much quieter than she remembered. She saw a young man sitting on the grass playing a guitar with about twenty people gathered around to listen, but the sound was not amplified and no one was carrying boom boxes or wearing Walkmans. She could hear birds twittering, water splashing in a fountain, and wind whispering through the trees.

"It's nice here," she said.

The MacBean grinned happily. "Och, lass, wait till you meet the mayor, you mon tell her."

The trolley stopped in front of Gracie Mansion, a graceful white house overlooking the East River. It looked pretty much the same as it did in Falcon's New York, though she wasn't sure whether it was smaller or whether it just seemed smaller because Carl Schurz Park was so much bigger.

"Here we are, dearios," said the driver, tipping his hat. They walked across the lawn to the front door and the MacBean rang the bell. They heard an awful ruckus from inside, many feet running, barking, meowing, squawking, and over it all a voice saying, "Oh dear! Oh mercy! I'm coming, I'm coming—oops! Tassy, you nearly tripped me up! Lordy, can they really be here already? Dear, oh mercy . . ."

The door flew open and there stood an enormous woman in a pair of striped overalls. She had a glorious mane of wiry black hair and brown eyes that peered through a pair of wire-rimmed glasses. She carried a French horn and a large blue parrot and was completely surrounded by four dogs of assorted breeds and sizes, six cats ditto, eight geese, five ducks, a cormorant that flapped onto the doorstep and made a mess on the MacBean's shoe, and a very young dragon the size of a chihuahua.

Falcon and Toody stared with all their might. There was something very familiar about the woman and Falcon wondered what it could be.

"I'll be off then, yer honor, and see to the café," said the MacBean, cleaning his shoe off on the grass. "Good luck to you, lassies and young laddy." He bowed and turned on his heel, whistling "Loch Lomond" as he went.

"Oh dear, Mr. MacBean," called the mayor after him. "I'm so sorry about that. Well, birds will be birds, you know, and let's see, where was I? Oh yes! Welcome, I am Calvurnia Rumple, mayor pro tem la-dee-dah etcetera of the great city of New York, blah blah and so forth. There, that's done, thank heavens. Now, what can I do for you?"

She ushered them into a sunny room whose windows faced the water. The lighthouse in the middle of the river that had been a crumbling ruin in Falcon's New York was all spruced up with well-tended flowerbeds and windows that sparkled in the sun. Toody stood looking out, fascinated by the river traffic. There were sailboats, of course, but he also saw a Chinese junk, a barge festooned with flowers and silk canopies, a gam of pilot whales and a pod of seals leaping through the waves. A large sea serpent in an officer's cap was herding several plesiosaurs toward Roosevelt Island while the lighthouse keeper's children cheered them on in shrill, piping voices and all sorts of birds soared and swooped above them, hunting the fish stirred up in their wake. There were gulls and skuas; jaegers, pelicans, and terns; cranes and avocets; cormorants like the one that had pooped on the MacBean; and a dozen dodos in a stately flotilla bobbing along on the current.

The animals trooped into the living room after the mayor, while the birds flapped and waddled through the French doors onto the lawn to nibble on the tender spring grass. The cats draped themselves on chair backs and laps, the dogs flopped down on the hearth rug, and the dragon perched on the andirons in the fireplace, emitting tiny snorts of steam whenever one of the dogs got too close. Falcon was interested to see that this infant dragon, unlike Egg, was bright blue with a silver crest.

The mayor sat in an armchair near the window.

"I was led to believe there was a dragon in your party?"

"Yes," said Falcon. "He's on his way."

"You knew we were coming?" asked Blinda.

"Oh yes, a little bird told me. I look forward to meeting your dragon," said the mayor. "We're very fond of them in these parts and there aren't many left. You have a great many in your world, I take it?"

"Oh, no," said Falcon. "We don't have any. At least I don't think we do, except for Dirus and Egg, of course. They're practically extinct. And if anyone found out about them, they would be."

The mayor looked puzzled, and when Falcon explained about keeping Egg a secret all last year, and how worried she had been about people finding out and turning the young dragon into a laboratory animal or a circus act, the mayor was terribly upset.

"Oh, mercy! Dear me, what a terrible tale!" she said, leaning back in her chair and fanning herself with a copy of *Cook's Illustrated*. "What a dreadful place you come from! Oh dear, no offense meant, I'm sure, but cruelty to animals—why, here, anyone who is cruel to an animal or a person is instantly banished to the Island of Mean."

Just at that moment, a little bird flew in the window and perched on Calvurnia's shoulder. It sang and twittered right in her ear as she nodded and scribbled in a large green notebook.

"Oh, my dears, I'm afraid there's some trouble with your dragon," said the mayor. "He's on his way here and he is very upset."

They all ran outside, and sure enough, there was Dirus flying low over the city, a most magnificent sight, his gray-green wings scarcely moving as he soared through the clear blue sky and landed right in front of the mayor, who looked delighted.

"Oh, welcome! Welcome!" she said, curtsying and

smiling. "I'm so happy to meet you, Lord Dirus, I do hope there's nothing very wrong; if there's anything at all we can do to help . . ."

The dragon, though he was in a great hurry and most anxious to talk with Falcon and Blinda, bowed politely. Dragons, no matter how fierce, are always courteous.

"Thank you, your honor," he said. "But I have grave news and cannot accept your kind offer until you hear what has happened."

Falcon thought the news must be very bad indeed, for she had never heard Dirus speak in prose before. When she glanced at Blinda, she saw that the witch had gone as white as milk.

"Oh, my friends," said Dirus, "a dreadful thing has transpired. I should have known when my head began to ache this afternoon, but I thought it was all that coffee. Egg has been discovered, and even now her freedom and maybe her very life are in terrible danger." He rubbed the side of his head, which was throbbing most painfully.

"What happened?" said Blinda, Falcon, and the mayor all together.

"A party of tourists from Minneapolis was crossing the Northern Territory in a bus; they took a wrong turn, blew a tire, and when they all got out, they saw Harry and Egg and . . . and the others building a hut beside the thimble."

"What thimble? What do you mean—what others?" said Blinda.

"The silver thimble. It's still making never-ending

coffee, and Harry's going to open a café. He was going to call it The Dragon's Cup." Dirus's ruby eyes filled with tears. "And Harry's people came to help." He sniffed. "And, oh my dears, your father is there, too. He came to find you."

"Peter?" cried Falcon. "Peter's there?"

"Yes," said Dirus. "He arrived just after we left. Now all kinds of other people are there: reporters, government officials, scientists, an Australian general and an American one, the commissioner in charge of food and beverage licenses, and several companies of soldiers and Marines. They're all shouting and arguing and waving guns, and there are TV cameras and . . ." Dirus gave a great sob as a fountain of tears exploded from his eyes, drenching everyone in a cool liquid that smelled of lilacs, as dragontears always do.

Toody stepped inside and fetched a tablecloth for Dirus to blow his nose on. He stood beside the dragon, patting his leg, which seemed to help, for Dirus pulled himself together and went on.

"I must get back and help them, find that space rift and fly through it right away—there's no time to lose."

The mayor shook her head, sending droplets of dragontears flying from her curly black hair.

"Easier said than done, my lord. The rift is unpredictable; you could wait for days before another one came along."

"My father!" said Falcon. "We have to save them; they

mustn't hurt Egg. She's, she's . . ." *This is all my fault*, she thought as tears threatened to overwhelm her in that infuriating way they had, just when she needed to be smart and strong. She bit the inside of her cheek and clenched her fists to keep from crying.

"Oh, Blinda, isn't there something you can do?"

Blinda looked at her. "Where there's a witch, there's a way, as my grandmother Ninda would say." She handed Falcon a large green handkerchief.

"Blow," she said.

CHAPTER
TWELVE

T OODY CLAMBERED UP DIRUS'S LEG AND SETTLED HIM-
self behind the dragon's head.

"Let's go," he said. "Let's get Missy; she'll fix it."

"Tood, we can't," said Falcon. "Missy isn't here, we're in the wrong New York, and anyway she—"

"Not Missy. Saint George," said Blinda. She began going through her pockets one by one, pulling out a mirror, a pork chop, two pencil stubs, a large jar of Tums, one red high-heeled sandal (size ten), a toy leopard, several English coins, a battered copy of *Classic Home Desserts* by Richard Sax, a half-eaten seven-ounce Hershey bar with almonds, a bag of pita bread, a banana, an old-fashioned rubber girdle, and a young manticore, who hissed and ran into the bushes.

"Saints, saints, let me see . . . not exactly what I wanted, but it'll have to do. Now then, here we are," she muttered, laying out the pork chop, the shoe, the leopard, a six-sided fifty-pence piece, a round of pita bread, the banana, the girdle, and a beautiful photograph of a Chocolate Cloud Cake from *Classic Home Desserts*.

Dirus snorted. "That's not it at all, you know; you've got it all wrong. It's supposed to be: dragon held captive in the princess's girdle, which means a *belt*, Saint George running in red-*hot* shoes, healing *lepers,* not leopards, and saints carry *banners*, not bananas, for Pete's sake. And what's that picture for, anyway?"

Blinda blushed. "It's so Saint George can see that Egg's enemies get their just desserts. It's the best I can do, my spell check isn't working, and everything comes out a little off."

"A little!" said Dirus. "And what about the red cross for the banner? Or in this case, the banana?"

Blinda rummaged through her pockets again and came up empty-handed.

"Oh, drat and double drat," she was saying when Toody, who had been paying close attention, scrambled down from Dirus's back and held out his leg. Two bright red Band-Aids were crisscrossed on his knee, just below the grimy cuff of his shorts.

"Splendiferous!" said Blinda. "Just the thing. Are you sure it's all right to take them off?"

"Yup," said Toody. "It's all scabby now." He picked at the edge of the bottom Band-Aid till both of them came off in one perfect cross-shaped piece, revealing a scab the size of a penny on his kneecap. They all stared at it for a minute.

"I fell," said Toody. "I didn't cry."

Blinda arranged the assorted objects into a pile on the grass, with the banana on top draped with the criss-crossed red Band-Aids. "All set," she said, stepping back. Dirus reared back, took a deep breath, and blew hard on the pile, but instead of a great blast of flame, a huge glob of dragon snot exploded from his nostrils, covering the pile in pale lavender slime.

"YUCK!" said Blinda, Falcon, and Calvurnia all together. Dirus was mortified. A dull blue blush spread over his face and neck.

"Oh dear, oh dear," he said, rubbing his forefeet together in distress. "I'm so sorry, it's been a long time, I just don't have it anymore. Oh, I am old, I am old, I wear the scales of my talons rolled . . ."

"Nonsense!" said the mayor, who knew that when a dragon starts misquoting T. S. Eliot, he's seriously depressed. "All you need is a little something to prime the pump." She went inside and returned with a large bottle of whiskey in each hand.

Dirus took the bottles and drank the contents one after the other. His color returned to normal and a warm red glow spread from his throat down to his chest, where his dragon heart beat true and brave and hot as blazes. Again he took a long breath, and this time a tremendous blast of fire engulfed Blinda's pile so that it burst into flame. A peculiar yet not unpleasant smell of burning banana, scorched pita bread, and roast pork rose from the bonfire, and as the flames died a tall cloud of gray smoke hid the patch of burnt grass from view.

As they watched, the smoke began to take shape. When it cleared, they wiped their watering eyes to see a tall, thin man of indeterminate age dressed in gray sweatpants, sneakers, and a hooded sweatshirt with a dancing dragon on the front over the motto SALTARE CUM DRACONIS.* His face was rosy and his straggly gray hair and eyebrows were frizzy, as though he had faced a good deal of dragon fire, and indeed he had. They heard a faint jingle as a golden disk the size of a dinner plate clinked onto the flagstone walk.

"Blasted halo!" said the saint, and he picked up the disk, sticking it on the back of his head, where it looked, thought Falcon, as if it would fall off any minute.

St. George smiled through a mouthful of crooked teeth. "Rumbustious journey, what?" he said, smoothing his windblown hair. "Bit of dragon bother, eh missy?"

Toody, who loved Aunt Emily's stories about the saint and had a picture of him in his bedroom, said, "Where's your armor?"

"Never wear it these days, young feller, me lad," said St. George, peering down at the little boy. "Awful stuff, itchy as blazes, heavy, rusts in the rain. Can't beat a good

*Saltare cum draconis (gloriosus est): "It is a glorious thing to dance with dragons."—Yarg Ilul, c. 1172

tracksuit and a pair of plimsolls for all-purpose wear, so practical and becoming, what?" He struck a pose and the halo fell off.

Dirus, who was still fired up by the whiskey and terribly worried about Egg, snorted a polite gush of flame and said, "Pardon me, your blessedness, but we have a most dreadful dilemma and beg your holy assistance, if you would be so kind?"

The saint, who was remarkably limber for someone 1,700 years old, sat cross-legged on the grass while Dirus told him what was happening in Australia and how Egg and Peter and Harry were in so much danger.

St. George grew very solemn as he listened, making sympathetic noises and shaking his head.

"Good lord, bit of tohubohu, what?" He twirled the halo absent-mindedly and then stuck it back on his head at a jaunty angle. At last he stood up, soldierly and stern-jawed. "There's nothing else for it, old beans," he said. "Won't be pleasant; dangerous, very, but it's the only way. Fax." He folded his arms, looking pleased with himself. The smile began to waver as they all looked blankly back at him, and his already pink face turned scarlet. "*Fax*, I say! Simple English, blast it!"

Calvurnia Rumple stepped forward, the highest-ranking person present, except for Dirus, who wasn't exactly a person.

"Excuse me, your saintliness," she said, "but if you mean fax as in fax machine, for sending messages, what exactly is it we're going to send?"

"Ourselves, of course," said the saint. "We send ourselves to Australia, one by one, through a fax machine."

Toody giggled. He knew about fax machines. He had tried to send his father a Fluffernutter sandwich through Ardene Taylor's fax. Ardene said it wasn't necessary for Missy to pay the repair bill, but Missy had insisted.

"You can't do that, Mr. George," he said. "They'll be mad and you'll have to go to your room."

Blinda's eyes were bright with excitement. "You know, it just might be possible! Bypass the space rift through the telephone lines."

"But wouldn't we come out all flat?" said Falcon, who didn't like the idea one bit. Sometimes the papers that went into Ardene's fax got jammed in the machine. She didn't want to be jammed. She began to think there was such a thing as too much magic.

"Of course we will, that's the danger, the peril, the fearful hazard, *yah ha!*" said St. George, waving an imaginary sword and thrusting at invisible enemies. "Take *that!*"

"I have a fax in my office," said Calvurnia.

"What about Dirus?" said Falcon. "He won't fit in your office."

"We'll do it out here," said the mayor. "With extension cords." Toody followed Calvurnia into the house. He loved anything that had to do with electricity.

"Blinda," said Falcon. She tugged at the witch's sleeve.

"Blinda!" The witch was searching the never-empty pockets of her jump suit. She pulled out a bowl of mulligatawny soup and paused.

"Yes, dear, what is it?"

Falcon picked at the skin on the side of her thumb. "Blinda, I . . . I don't . . . that is, do you really think it's a good idea to go through the fax machine? I mean, Saint George said we'd come out all flat and then what do we do? And what if we get . . ." She gulped. "What if we get *mangled?*"

Blinda's eyes seemed to look right through her.

"It's all right to be afraid, Falcon, as long as it doesn't stop you from doing what you have to do. Here, this'll put hair on your chest." She handed Falcon the soup and went back to searching her pockets.

Falcon sat with the bowl of soup in her hands. She wasn't hungry, and anyhow soup out of Blinda's pockets might actually put hair on her chest. She remembered how brave and calm she always felt when she looked into Egg's deep blue eyes and tried to get that feeling back. She hoped none of the others would find out what a coward she was.

CHAPTER
THIRTEEN

WHILE FALCON AND HER FRIENDS WERE GETTING ready to fax themselves to Australia, Egg, Harry, and Peter were completely surrounded by a mob of people and machines. Harry's clan had slipped away and were watching from a safe distance up the beach. Soldiers, trucks, and an armored tank were lined up near the three of them, guns drawn. Four news helicopters had landed, and a dozen journalists with microphones were rushing about followed by cameramen, cameras, and producers with clipboards and expensive sunglasses. Several of the journalists were interviewing assorted experts: military, scientific, and an editor from *The Skeptical Inquirer*, who was saying, "There is as yet no proof that this is, in fact, a dragon. Further tests will have to be conducted before any final determination can be made . . ."

A talk show host had set up several rows of chairs

facing Egg and was talking to a psychic with dyed blond hair and a big bosom. "Of course," she said, "I predicted all of this, if people would have only listened."

An anthropologist, two zoologists, the curator of the Melbourne Zoo, fourteen firefighters, twenty-seven policemen, a taxidermist, three film directors, and the tour guide were milling around, getting in each other's way and arguing. Most of the arguments had to do with who owned the dragon. Near the shore, three fishing boats, a research vessel from Sydney Marine Biology Centre, and a nuclear submarine floated just beyond the surf. At least twenty people were paddling about on rubber rafts and surfboards while a crazed lifeguard screamed at them to get out of the water. Another helicopter landed, and a short man dressed in camouflage gear jumped out and ran across the beach to a point about twenty yards from Egg. The man peered at the dragon through the binoculars that hung round his neck.

"Dragon my Aunt Fanny!" he said, staring. He adjusted a small microphone clipped to his lapel and spoke into it, watching Egg the whole time. His lips hardly moved as he spoke, and his voice was surprisingly deep and resonant for such a small man.

"Burton T. Goody," he said. "The voice of true blue Americans everywhere, coming to you from a beach on the Arafura Sea in northwestern Australia, with the facts about this so-called dragon. Remember, it takes a real man to tell you the real American truth!" He switched off the tape recorder. Overhead a small plane swooped low over the beach to get a better look, making everyone duck and shout angrily at the sky. Burton T. Goody frowned. "Dragon! Hooey!" he said.

In the middle of this Harry sat cross-legged beside the ever-flowing cappuccino bowl. He was chanting softly and tapping out a rhythm on the rim of the bowl with a tea-spoon.

Peter stood as close to the dragon as he could, arms folded across his chest. He had a slight sunburn from her heat, and his nose was beginning to peel.

Egg sat on her haunches at the edge of the sea, flames flickering along her crest. Now and then a hiss of steam rose into the air as a wavelet brushed her burning hide.

"I wish I could tell Falcon how sorry I am," said Peter.

"Oft thy displeasure, that was so unjust, did grieve thy daughter so to lose thy trust," said Egg in a low voice.

"I yelled at her; I've never yelled at her before." He walked over to one of the policemen to try and get him to call off the crowd, but the officer just said, "Sorry, sir, I have my orders." An army captain and a journalist were no help either; nobody would listen.

Peter hunkered down beside Harry and looked up at Egg.

"They're never going to let you go, are they?" he said.

"They would be masters of what is not their own," said Egg. "When troubles come, they come not single spies, but in battalions."

"Too right, luv," said Harry, handing Peter a mug of cappuccino. "Sugar?"

Peter shook his head.

"Missy tried to tell me about Egg last year but I just laughed at her. And Falcon. She told me the truth, and I . . ." He rubbed his hand across his eyes.

"What is done cannot be now amended; men do speak unwisely sometimes," said the dragon.

Harry peered at the crowd milling around at a safe distance from the dragon. "Look, luv, suppose you just blow a good blast of fire over their heads, give 'em a scare, create a diversion. Then we could run out of range and you could take off."

Egg shook her head and said, "It would folly be to hazard you for me." She didn't mention the other problem: Dragons, once they are past infancy, can't rise quickly into the air like helicopters. They need room to make a running start, and though they are strong, swift fliers, they are slow on takeoff. Harry, even though he was a shaman, didn't seem to know this, and Egg was too shy to tell him. She was a young dragon and painfully self-conscious.

"Never mind, luv. I'm sure Dirus and Blinda and the kiddies will hear my song and bring help." Harry returned to his chanting, and Peter, who knew a lot of Aboriginal chants, soon joined him, their song rising into the still air on the sparks from Egg's fiery crest. It made a kind of calm in the middle of all the hubbub.

CHAPTER
FOURTEEN

IN PARALLEL NEW YORK, BLINDA AND CALVURNIA WERE
setting up the fax machine on the flagstone terrace in
a tangle of extension cords and duct tape. Toody was
helping. St. George was sitting under a tree with Dirus,
eating the mulligatawny soup and discussing their dancing
days.

"I would have won the cup, you know," said Dirus, "if
those judges hadn't called for the Shim Sham. I wasn't
expecting that, it was so unfair."

"You could have done it, old sock. It's all a matter of
confidence and remembering left and right. Look." The
saint got up and began hopping and kicking while Dirus
looked on. After a minute the dragon began humming
"The Shim Sham" and copying St. George, who was
chanting, "Turn, hop, shuffle back, back, slide right, hop!"

Falcon sat watching the mayor and the witch fiddle

with the fax. It looked like a very jerrybuilt setup, with three extension cords and the yards of duct tape Toody was plastering over everything. She was sure it wouldn't work, or if it did that it would be extremely dangerous. All she wanted was to go home with Toody. *I'm sick of this*, she thought, clenching her fists. *I want to be back home with Missy and just be normal!*

"You can't," said Blinda, as though she had read Falcon's mind.

"What do you mean? I didn't say anything," said Falcon.

"You didn't have to, dearie, it's all there on your face, plain as day. Not that your face is plain, not at all, though we might do something about that hair, a French braid maybe? Comb!" The witch rummaged in her pocket and pulled out a pistachio ice cream cone. "*Comb*, I said, c-o-m-b! Oh, what's the use, here, have it, I'm trying to cut down." She handed Falcon the ice cream cone. After more searching she found a large, amber plastic bottle. "Aha! There it is! I knew it was in there somewhere." She sat down beside Falcon, who was licking the ice cream without much enthusiasm. She preferred strawberry. "Don't you want it, dear?" said Blinda. "Oh well, mustn't go to waste." She took the cone and bit off the end, pushing the ice cream down with her tongue and sucking it noisily out the bottom.

"What did you mean?" said Falcon. "Did you mean we *can't* go home?"

"Oh no, dear, I expect we'll get home eventually, well,

if this fax thing works and we're not killed in the battle," said Blinda cheerfully, licking ice cream off her fingers.

"Battle!" said Falcon. "What battle, I don't want to be in a battle, nobody said anything about a battle, I thought we were just going to rescue them, what battle?"

"Goodness, what a fuss!" said Blinda. "You don't imagine all those people are going to let Egg go without a fight, do you? There's nothing to worry about, we've got Dirus and Saint George. Then there's me, of course," she said rather smugly. "And . . ." The witch peered at Falcon with her x-ray eyes. "There's a lot more to you than you know. That's what I meant."

"I think we're all set," said the mayor. The fax machine, not dull gray like the ones in our world but pink with purple stripes, sat on the terrace festooned with cords, blue duct tape, and a few raisins from Calvurnia's excellent rice pudding. Apart from the color it looked very like the one in Ardene's office (before the Fluffernutter), and Falcon didn't see how any of them, let alone Dirus, were going to go through it. Her mouth was dry and tasted horribly of pistachios. She tried to think of courageous women who had faced danger and triumphed. Rosa Parks. Boudicca. Joan of Arc. She saw St. Joan tied to a stake with flames reaching for her legs. "Oh no," she muttered. "Not her, not Joan."

"Beryl Markham," said Blinda. "Madame Curie, Harriet Tubman, Emmeline Pankhurst, Ida B. Wells, Florence Nightingale, Edith Cavell."

Before Falcon could say, *who*? Blinda had turned away

to join the others. "It's inside you, Falcon," she said over her shoulder.

What's inside me? Falcon wondered. She didn't think anything was inside her except all those slimy red and blue parts she'd seen in her biology book.

Dirus and St. George were arguing about who should be faxed first.

"I should go first, I'm the oldest and the biggest. If it works for me, it'll work for any of you," said the dragon.

"I am a warrior and a knight," said St. George, "*and* a saint, and winner of the Latin American specialties dance contest six years running. You called me up, you invoked me from the dim and dusky maelstrom of myth, and what for but to lead this glorious enterprise clad in the shining armor of righteousness and—"

"Oh piffle," said Blinda. "I have these." She held up the large amber bottle she had pulled out of her pocket and read the label aloud: "'Dr. Quacker's Bolus Bombasticus, All Natural, Contains only extract of bloviating senators in a base of braggadocio and smugwort. Take with a grain of salt.' These are antisqueeze pills. You'll have to take them to reinflate yourselves when you come out of the fax machine. And only a licensed and registered witch can administer them, so I will go first."

"Who's going to give *you* the pills, then?" asked St. George.

"I don't need 'em," said Blinda. "I'm a witch. I can inflate myself."

After a good deal more argument, it was finally decided. Blinda would go first, then Dirus, then St. George, and the children last.

By this time Falcon had bitten all her fingernails down to the quick, and Toody had run out of blue duct tape and had eaten the last of the rice pudding. He came over to his sister and peered into her face.

"I have some gum," he said. "You can have it if you want." He pulled a wad of gum from his pocket and handed it to Falcon. "I only chewed it a little," he said.

"Thanks, Tood," said Falcon. "I'll save it for later."

"Come along, you two," said Blinda. "We're going." She led them to where the others were standing around the fax machine. They heard a loud twittering as a chickadee landed on Calvurnia's shoulder and chattered shrilly in her ear as she nodded and said, "Really? Oh, excellent, well done." The bird flew off and the mayor said, "It's all set. The shaman sang up a vision of you in the sparks from Egg's fire. One of his cousins has arranged a fax machine to receive you out of sight of the crowd."

"Good old Harry," said Blinda. "Let's get started."

She turned to Falcon and Toody. "All right. You stick together and come along after St. George. There's no need to fear, just trust in yourselves and your sturdy shoes. There's nothing like comfortable shoes in a battle."

The witch turned and switched on the fax machine, which began to vibrate and hum. Then she put the bottle of antisqueeze pills back in her pocket, took a deep breath, and bent over. Falcon shut her eyes. She heard a rhythmic *ka-chunk-a-chunk* that went on for several minutes. At last, since she didn't hear any screaming, she opened her eyes. Blinda had vanished and the others were standing around the machine talking excitedly. Toody's eyes were round as Frisbees.

"Falcon, she went into the fax all flat. Is Blinda going to see Egg?" he asked, tugging at her hand.

"Good heavens, she did it!" said Calvurnia. "You should have seen it, my dear; slick as a whistle, quite amazing."

"Now then," said Dirus, and he lowered his scaly head. This time Falcon made herself watch. Sure enough, the minute the dragon's head touched the slot of the fax, he seemed to shrink and flatten into a smooth gray-green sheet that slipped easily inside until all that remained was the arrowhead tip of his long tail. It gave one final twitch and vanished into the machine.

St. George was next, and like the knightly dancer he was he struck an elegant pose, pointed his right foot in its gray sneaker, and chasséd himself into the fax, where he disappeared, toes pointed to the last.

Toody tugged at Falcon's hand, pulling her toward the table. "Our turn, Falcon, let's go."

Falcon stretched her lips into a smile for Toody's benefit, squeezed his hand, and said, "Okay, Tood, let's go see Peter and Egg."

The children laid their heads flat on the table against the mouth of the fax machine. Just before it began, Falcon remembered a picture she had seen in a book about Mary Queen of Scots. The doomed queen was kneeling with her head flat on the block and her arms outstretched, about to have her head chopped off for treason. Then Falcon felt a gentle tug on her hair and a kind of delicious tingling through her neck and shoulders, like the feeling you get when you have a really good catlike stretch first thing in the morning. She closed her eyes at the last moment, and when she opened them, she couldn't see anything but blackness punctuated by flashes of light like fireworks. The *ka-chunk-a-chunk* sound was quite loud, and she still felt Toody's hand, like a small warm animal, in her own.

After a few minutes the darkness lightened gradually into sunshine and bright blue sky. Falcon felt limp and relaxed and quite unable to move. She seemed to be lying on the ground, and she heard birds calling and a sort of rumbling in the distance.

"Well done, you two!" said a familiar voice, and Blinda's face loomed over them. "Here, swallow this." She pushed a small pill between Falcon's lips along with a single grain of salt and immediately Falcon felt as though her insides were being blown up by an air pump the way they blow up helium balloons at the five-and-dime. It got so uncomfortable she began to think she was going to explode with the biggest belch in the universe when Blinda said, "Well, breathe, for heaven's sake!" So she did, and energy flooded into her flat body. As she began to reinflate, the giant belch feeling went away and she saw a flat Toody beside her slowly rounding out into his normal little-boy shape. When she sat up, there were the others, bending and stretching, hopping and swinging their arms to get the last bits of flatness out of their bones. They greeted her and each other with great joy, and for the first time she felt a part of them, now that she had done something she feared and had come through alive. Somewhere deep inside her a clear blue drop of courage began to grow.

"We happy few, we band of brothers, eh what?" said St. George.

"And sisters!" said Blinda. "We've still got *that* to deal with."

She pointed through the trees at the distant beach and they all looked. *So that's what the rumbling was,* thought Falcon as she stared at the crowd of people, cars, trucks, and equipment littering the sand in a shifting semicircle around the central figure of Egg. Even from a quarter-mile away she could see the glow of dragonfire. Egg looked small against the vastness of sea and sky, and she remembered how tiny the dragon had been when she first hatched.

"They won't get you, Egg," she whispered fiercely. "I won't let them." She saw Harry, too, a dark shape hunkered down near a half-built shack, and then she saw Peter.

"Daddy!" she cried. The embattled three turned toward the sound and she caught the flash of the dragon's beautiful turquoise eyes.

"Hush!" said St. George. "The mob'll spy us out."

"No they won't," said Blinda. "They're making too much noise of their own. Dragons and shamans have very sharp ears. And fathers, too."

"Now then, chaps," said St. George, "here's the plan, what? Dirus, this is a bit dicey for you but I don't reckon they'll shoot as you are such a rare and spiffy creature." The dragon turned his head modestly and blushed a deep cerulean blue.

"You stroll forward toward the crowd. The rest of us will conceal ourselves under your belly and behind your wings, carrying musical instruments. Then when attention has been distracted away from Egg to you, we start infiltrating the crowd. At my signal everyone begins to play and I'll call the dance, until—"

"The *dance?*" said Falcon. "What do you mean? Those people want to put Egg in a zoo, they've got guns—dancing won't help."

The saint gave her a cold look. "I beg your pardon, missy, who's the soldier and the dragon expert here, I'd like to know?"

Falcon whispered to the witch so as not to upset St. George.

"Blinda, can't you do like before and turn the guns to chocolate?" The witch looked embarrassed.

"I don't exactly know how, Falcon. That was a sort of . . . mistake."

Falcon gritted her teeth. *Even magical grownups are no help; I'll have to do it myself,* she thought, though she wasn't quite sure at the moment what "it" might be.

"Ms. Cholmondely," said the saint, "can you supply us with instruments?

Blinda concentrated for a few minutes, eyes closed. Then she reached into her pockets and pulled out a kazoo, a small drum, a saxophone, and a tambourine. She looked immensely pleased and said, "There now, see what you can do when you pay attention!"

"What about you, Dirus?" said the saint. "You'll want all your feet for dancing, but would you like a harmonica, perhaps, or a kazoo?"

The old dragon shook his head proudly. "I," he said, "shall sing."

"Splendid," said St. George, looking rather dubious. "Is everyone ready? At my signal—now then, left, right, left, right, on we go and watch for my cue."

The great gray-green dragon ambled forward out of the forest with Blinda under one wing carrying the sax, Toody and Falcon (drum and kazoo) under the lowest part of the dragon's belly as they were the shortest, and St. George on tambourine in the lead just under the dragon's chest.

It took a while before anyone noticed Dirus because they were all facing in the other direction, toward Egg. Finally the old dragon said, *AHEM!*" and a small boy in the audience of the *Sally Sue Summer Show* yelled, "Whoa! There's another dragon!" Heads began to turn and the rumbling grew to a roar as more and more people saw the huge dragon, many times larger than Egg, standing only twenty feet from the edge of the crowd.

There was a small riot as half the people scrambled to get closer and the other half tried to get as far away as possible. Gradually the crowd calmed down as people realized that this dragon did not seem to be burning hot at the moment and he was staying where he was and making no sudden movements. Most of the crowd gradually turned away from Egg and gathered around Dirus, at a safe distance. The soldiers and Marines did not move since they had been given no orders, but they did swivel their heads around to see what everyone was looking at. This was a dangerous thing to do, because as anyone who knows about guns will tell you, a person holding a gun tends to point it in the direction he is looking. Burton T. Goody did not turn his head, but he could see what was happening out of the corners of his cold gray eyes. He heard the chaos behind him, and noticed how careless the soldiers were with their weapons. A thin smile touched his lips.

"Fools," he said, never taking his eyes off Egg.

St. George raised his hands and the crowd grew quiet. The musicians waited for their cue.

"Play!" said the saint, and they did, starting off with "Good Golly Miss Molly" and going on to "Mambo Italiano," "Susie's Rag," and the waltz from *La Traviata*. The saint called the tunes and the dances, too, and there must have been magic in those instruments, which seems only natural as they came out of the pockets of a pretty good, fully licensed and registered, certified, genuine witch. People listened and relaxed and then perked up. Toes began tapping, fingers snapping, hands clapping. Soon everyone was gliding and striding, strutting and hopping, swaying and bopping, swinging, dancing, turning, prancing, bucking, flouncing, jigging, bouncing to the irresistible, ticklesome, teasing tunes of the Saint George Dragon Band! Above the fine brassy sound of sax, tambourine, drum, and kazoo rose the glorious voice of Dirus, that most ancient and melodious dragon, adding a trill here and a warble there, now tenor, now bass.

St. George was everywhere, leading the dance, his face red with excitement, his sneakers scarcely touching the ground.

"Right foot, left foot, swing it round; hayfoot, strawfoot, up and down. Wave your arms and don't be slow, find your fella for a do-si-do. Jump and shimmy, strut and swing; come on, mama, shake that thing! Clap your hands and do that strut; wiggle your nose and bounce that butt! One big circle, spin and twirl; hand in hand around the world!"

Falcon, who had been trying to think of how she could save Peter and Egg, began to wonder whether the saint's plan might actually succeed. She blew her kazoo as hard as she could on a particularly tricky bit of "The Chapel Hill Stomp."

On and on they danced. Soldiers, sailors, and Marines dropped their weapons one by one till there was a huge pile on the sand. Round and round they circled: politicians and journalists; bureaucrats and scientists; tourists and gawkers; the man selling souvenir T-shirts and the preacher with his collar askew all danced together while Harry led his people back to their village, leaving Egg and Peter by the edge of the sea looking on.

In all the joyful hullabaloo, no one noticed when the small man in camouflage gear picked up a discarded M-16 rifle and turned his back on the dancers. He seemed to stand taller, holding the gun.

"Ten-hut!" he said, and spoke into the microphone, neck rigid, eyes fixed on Egg and Peter.

"I claim this hyped-up overgrown lizard, dead or alive, for the good old Yoo Ess of Ay," he said. "And for real men everywhere." He took a deep breath, sticking out his chest, and pointed the gun at Egg. She blazed against the sky, hot enough to melt lead, and Goody swore under his breath. Then he shifted the rifle just a few inches to one side. He looked through the sight at Peter's chest and smiled his chilly smile. "*Now* I've got you," he said.

CHAPTER
FIFTEEN

THE DANCE WENT ON AND ON AS THE MOON ROSE AND the stars came out. Mothers and fathers picked up their sleepyhead toddlers and went on dancing with the babies cradled against them. Tired children staggered to the edge of the crowd and fell asleep on the sand. Old folk heard half-forgotten memories in the dragon's song and felt the years slip away from their jigging feet, while teenagers forgot themselves altogether and danced with their own parents.

The four musicians played and Dirus sang untiring as the night wore on and the sky began to lighten. And in all this happiness and music and laughter there were only three who neither danced nor sang.

On the shore, Peter stood in front of Egg, still and silent. Burton T. Goody stood facing them, pointing his rifle straight at Peter's heart. He had not turned his head once to watch the dancers, nor did he tap his toes to the tempting tunes of the Saint George Dragon Band.

"Yond Goody hath a mean and angry look. He thinks too much. Such men are dangerous," said Egg.

Peter answered out of the side of his mouth; he didn't want to startle Goody. "He doesn't believe in you, but he wants to own you. Couldn't you scorch him a bit with that breath of yours?"

"I fear my furnace be so hot that it may but your own self burn, or dragon's flame consume him not, he will but fire in return," said Egg.

"If you could get him to look into your eyes," said Peter, who had learned a lot about dragons in the past few hours, "wouldn't that stop him?"

This was certainly true. Anyone who looks directly into the eyes of a dragon will see his own true self reflected there and be held in that magical gaze until the dragon chooses to release him. But try as she might, Egg could not attract Goody's attention. She snorted blasts of fire into the sky, she thrashed her burning tail, she arched her flaming wings till the air around her rippled with heat, but Burton T. Goody never took his eyes off Peter or moved his rifle even one centimeter off its target. He seemed to be aware of the music and laughter behind him only as you would be aware of the sound of distant traffic.

Dirus was taking a break after a truly soulful version of James Brown's "I Feel Good" while the band swung into "Take the 'A' Train" with Blinda blowing a mean sax.

The old dragon looked over at Peter, Egg, and Burton T. Goody, the three of them silhouetted against the glow of dragonfire on the dark sky.

"Falcon," he said. She was playing her kazoo full blast and didn't hear him at first. "Falcon." She took the kazoo out of her mouth and stepped closer to Dirus. "It's time," he said.

"Time for what?" said Falcon. She raised the kazoo to her lips. "Everyone's dancing and happy."

"Not everyone," said Dirus.

Falcon followed Dirus's gaze toward the sea and the three still figures.

"He's going to fire that gun in a minute," said Dirus. "He wants Egg, dead or alive."

"But he can't kill Egg with a gun, the bullets would melt before they hit her, and she would burn him up," said Falcon.

"He's not aiming at Egg." Falcon looked again and saw that this was true. She glared at Goody as though she could kill him with her eyes.

"Your father thinks no one would shoot him to get to Egg, but he's wrong," said the dragon. "Think, Falcon. Remember."

Remember what? she thought, still staring at Goody. "It's inside you," Blinda had said. What was *it*? Egg's bright scales glittered in the light of her own fire. Suddenly Falcon remembered the parades marching along Fifth Avenue with the sun flashing off the brass. She and Peter loved parades and marching bands and she remembered how, when she was little, before the divorce, she used to sit high on her father's shoulders to watch them, with her hands around his neck. He would take her hands in his and clap them together in rhythm to the sound of the drums, and she remembered how warm his hands were and the way his hair always smelled like toast. Music rose in her head: snare drums and trumpets, silver flutes and golden horns. She hummed a few bars.

"That's it!" said Dirus. "Now then, listen carefully . . ." He bent his long snaky neck down so his head was even closer to her own and whispered to her as she nodded, twisting the kazoo between her fingers.

Falcon and the dragon moved to the edge of the crowd, Dirus being careful not to squash anybody with his enormous feet or bash them with his tail. The band was playing "The Tennessee Waltz" as couples swayed dreamily to the sweet sound, eyes half closed with sleepiness.

"One of my favorites," said Dirus. "I was dancing with my darling dum de dum dum de dum dum . . ."

They halted twenty yards behind Burton T. Goody.

"Go on, young bird, don't stop to wave. Fortune favors, if you're brave," said Dirus.

"But what if . . . ?" said Falcon.

"Time rushes on, life passes by. What if? If only. . . . Fools do cry. March forth, good Falcon, don't delay, and carpe diem: Seize the day!"

He's so bossy, thought Falcon, taking a step forward. *And a rotten poet.*

Her stomach felt as though it were full of snakes, coiling and heaving, and a thin, sharp voice seemed to whisper in her ear: *You're only a little girl, and he has a gun. You can't do anything—look how scared you are. You can't even keep Toody safe; how can you save Peter from a man with a gun? You're just a cowardy-custard kid.*

It's true, thought Falcon, *it's all true.* She shut her eyes, wishing she could go to sleep and wake up in her own room at home to find this had all been a dream. She could hear the music behind her and the voices of the dancers, singing along. Underneath she heard the wind in the trees and the shushing sound of the sea. There were smells, too, of sweat and saltwater, of Harry's coffee and the clean, hot, spicy smell of dragonfire. The ring on her finger glowed and warmed her icy hand, and she remembered what she had seen when she looked into the clear blue depths of Egg's beautiful eyes.

"It's inside me," she whispered. She took a deep breath, squared her shoulders, and began to walk across the sand toward the rigid form of Burton T. Goody. She was twenty feet away from him when she spoke, in a small, sweet, little-girl voice.

"Excuse me, sir?" He tensed for a moment at the sound of her voice and then relaxed as he realized it was only a kid. He answered without turning his head.

"What is it?"

Instead of speaking, Falcon began to play her kazoo, very softly and slowly. Goody shook his head, not sure he was hearing what he heard. The tune infiltrated his mind, played so faintly he had to strain to hear it as the familiar words began to rise from his memory like smoke. "From the Halls of Montezuma to the shores of Tripoli . . ."

He gripped the rifle so hard his knuckles turned white, trying to hear the tune over the noise of dancers and ocean waves.

"Louder!" he hissed. Obediently, the tune strengthened and speeded up gradually to a marching beat.

"I coulda been a Marine, I coulda . . . if only . . . ," he whispered. His eyes glistened, and his feet began to move, lifting off the sand: one, two, three, four; hut, two, three, four; hut, two, hut, two . . .

Burton T. Goody stood at attention, shouldered his rifle, made a neat about-face, and marched off behind Falcon, who was playing "The Marine's Hymn" as loud as she could on Blinda's magical kazoo. As they approached the crowd, the band joined in: Toody, red in the face, beat his drum *a-rat-a-tat-tat*, with the *ching-ching-chingle* of St. George's tambourine and underneath it all the lowdown, funky sound of Blinda on that shining tenor sax—yes*sir*, to stir the soul and wake the dead, set their feet a-marchin' and a-struttin' proud as Old Glory!

The crowd stopped dancing and stood silent, no longer sleepy. The dozing children opened their eyes and sat up. Everybody gathered in a semicircle around Dirus and watched Falcon and Burton T. Goody come marching across the beach.

The sky was beginning to lighten but the moon and

stars still shone bright. Their cool glow touched the gray-green scales of the old dragon, lending a silvery glitter to his enormous bulk. He stood perfectly still, waiting, like a cat before a mousehole, and the arrowhead tip of his tail twitched slightly, right left, right left.

They drew near, Falcon playing with all her might. Her face shone pale in the moonlight as she stepped to one side to give Goody a clear path. The band came to the end of the song and fell silent.

Dirus lowered himself to the sand, his ancient joints creaking. His huge head stretched out before him as he opened his jaws wide, wider, widest into a black cavern rimmed with gleaming teeth, while the fierce red glow of his dragon heart burned up through the tunnel of his throat.

On and on marched Burton T. Goody, till there was no escape, no turning back, and he looked at last into the eyes of the dragon. His own eyes widened as he gazed, held by the double reflection of himself standing ramrod straight and strutting, square-jawed, shoulders back, a real he-man. "He-man," whispered Burton T. Goody, staring at his twin selves in the dragon's eyes with the dreadful darksome road of that ghastly gullet yawning before him. "A real he-man," he said again. "He-man!" Suddenly he snorted. "Heeee-man," he said, and giggled. "Hee-hee-hee-man! Hee-hee-haw-haw-ha-ha!" he chortled, dropping his rifle. "Troo-bloo-hoo-ha-ha-hooah-ha-he, oh I can't stand it!" He doubled over, clutching his belly, and roared with laughter at himself, howled and whooped helplessly, rolling on the sand, till everyone began to catch it. They caught laughter like the flu, shaking and howling, sinking down slowly in a grand, ridiculous earthquake of laughter at the wonderful, glorious absurdity of their own silly selves.

Peter turned to see Falcon running toward him and he caught her as she hurled herself into his arms.

"Falcon!" he cried. "Oh, my bird! My bird! My brave, brave girl."

"I was afraid!" she cried into his chest. "I almost didn't—"

"But you did it anyway, and even when no one believed you, you told the truth. Oh, my bird, I am so sorry." He put a finger under her chin and tilted her head up so he could look into her eyes.

"Can you forgive me?" he said. She nodded, unable to speak, and gave him a smile that was a little shaky at the edges. They walked hand in hand back to where the others had gathered around Dirus, who had curled his foretalons under his chest like a cat. Peter, Falcon, and the rest of the Saint George Dragon Band leaned against his warm scaly hide in the morning chill. Toody, still carrying his drumsticks, went off to see Harry.

Egg turned her clear eyes on Falcon. "Your goodness hath been great to me. I shall remember what you've bravely done."

"I couldn't let them hurt you, Egg," said Falcon. She remembered the night she decided to let Egg go free and seemed to see again the young dragon rising into the dark winter sky, higher and higher, till she brushed the moon with her wing. The smooth circle of moonsilver on Falcon's finger felt as warm as it had that night, new forged by dragonfire. She smiled. "A dragon has to be free," she said.

"My liberty plucks Goody by the nose," said Egg. She held Falcon in her cool blue gaze for a moment longer and then let her go.

Harry came strolling across the sand, carrying a sign that read THE DRAGON'S CUP: COFFEE, TEA, SANDWICHES. He set it down against the shack and stretched. The sky behind him had turned pearly pink and gray, and birds were calling over the sea.

Egg waddled over to stand near Dirus, who was one of her heroes. They watched the crowd, which was beginning to sober up, lying in heaps all limp and gasping, with an occasional aftershock chortle rippling through them. Several people had wet their pants from laughing, but nobody seemed to mind, and some of the children had hiccups, which made them giggle. Everybody felt floppy and happy and hopeful about everything for no particular reason.

"You did jolly well, Falcon," said St. George.

"Intrepid, remarkable child," rumbled Dirus, blinking tears out of his ruby eyes. He was very susceptible to sentimental family scenes.

Falcon smiled happily, then she remembered. "But Egg, what about you? It's not safe for you, even here in the Outback. Where will you go?"

"What about Parallel New York?" said Blinda. "They love dragons there. Egg, do you think you can find the space rift and fly through it?"

"A true devoted dragon is not feary to measure universes with her flaming flight," said Egg.

"Does that mean you'll do it?" said St. George, who had no patience with Egg's mangled Shakespeare.

"Yes," said Egg.

Most of the dancers had gone home, except for some reporters. They began asking Egg how she would get through the rift.

"On such a full sky shall we be aloft that we must take the current when it serves," said Egg.

Two of the reporters wrote this down in their notebooks. Falcon noticed that one of them spelled "current" with an "a." The third was a TV journalist named Andrea Crettin, and when she thrust her microphone into Egg's face, the dragon was so startled that she gasped, melting the mike into a blob and scorching Andrea's nail polish. Egg was terribly embarrassed by this and spent the next half-hour making sure that Ms. Crettin got all the information she wanted, rather a waste of time as there was no way to record it.

The odd thing was that later, when Ms. Crettin and the other reporters got back to their hotel, they couldn't quite remember what they'd seen. Their notes were illegible except for an excellent recipe for currant jam and a rather nice drawing of Harry's Dragon's Cup Café. The photographer's film showed the beach at various times of day, and Harry's café was clearly visible in the background, with a few tourists eating sandwiches and drinking iced cappuccino.

Falcon and the others noticed that none of the people on the beach was paying the slightest attention to them anymore.

"Fog of Forgetfulness," said Blinda. "They won't remember anything that's happened. One of my best spells, if I do say so myself."

At last it was time to say goodbye. Toody and Harry came back from the café, and everybody hugged everybody and cried a little.

"Goodbye, goodbye! Parting is such sweet sorrow, but I must say goodbye, not knowing of the morrow," said Egg, her seahorse head enveloped in a cloud of lilac-scented steam from her own tears.

Falcon could not speak at all, though she knew the dragon would be much better off in Parallel New York, where she would be loved and admired instead of hunted. She could only hold out a hand to the dragon's heat, wondering if she would ever see her again. Egg gazed at her with cool turquoise eyes.

"Who knows when we shall meet again, in summer lightning or in rain," she said. The ring on Falcon's finger tingled and seemed to shimmer before her eyes as Egg spoke. The young dragon gathered herself up and ran about thirty yards along the shore, gaining speed and making a smooth turn as she headed back toward the seven friends. She took off and skimmed over their heads, then she rose and circled once, trailing waves of heat as she flew. Falcon's eyes filled with tears and her voice came out in a strangled squeak. "Goodbye, Egg! Goodbye!" she cried, waving with both arms.

"Remember, arch your humerus into the updraft!" called Dirus as Egg dipped one wing in farewell and took off into the rising sun.

They watched and waved until the flaming dragon disappeared into the pale morning sky, and then everyone gave a great sigh and wiped their eyes.

"Lookit your ring, Falcon — it's got words!" said Toody.

They all looked, and sure enough, etched on the surface of the ring, three words glowed golden against the moonsilver.

"A Friend Indeed," Peter read. "Well!" He beamed at Falcon so proudly that she felt as though dragonfire were warming her face again.

"Excuse me?" said a voice. A small man in baggy shorts and an oversize T-shirt with a picture of a koala on it stood a little way off, looking shy. Falcon stepped forward, the hair on the back of her neck bristling like an angry cat's.

"You!" she said. "What do *you* want?"

Goody blushed and hung his head. "I only wanted to say . . . that is." He gulped. "I'm so sorry." He straightened his shoulders and spoke directly to Peter. "I owe you for all the trouble I've caused," he said. "If I can help you, sir, in any way, well, here's my card." He handed a business card to Peter, who looked at it before tucking it into his shirt pocket. It read: BURTON T. GOODY, TRUE BLUE AMERICAN HE-MAN, STAR OF RADIO STATION WMAN IN SHEBOYGAN, WI. Everything but the name and phone number had been crossed out. Goody turned to Falcon.

"Miss Davies," he said, "there's nothing more I can say but that I am truly sorry, and here's my hand." She hesitated but took the little man's hand at last and shook it. He made a stiff bow to the others, started to salute, thought better of it, turned, and walked off down the beach.

"Reformed sinner, eh what?" said St. George, shaking his head. "Time will tell, dontcha know." He picked the halo up and twirled it thoughtfully before sticking it back on his head. Dirus cleared his throat.

"Well! Now then, who's coming? Just climb aboard and fly with me, we'll soon be home in NYC."

Falcon, Blinda, Peter, and Toody climbed aboard and settled themselves on Dirus's broad scaly back; St. George sat in front. He was going to make a brief stopover in New York. "I want to pick up some chopped liver and bialys before I go back," he said. "You just can't get good deli in Heaven."

In addition to the excellent provisions he had packed, Harry also supplied Dirus with two tanks, one full of endless cappuccino to keep the old dragon awake on the trip, the other full of pawpaw juice for the others. Harry had rigged the tanks very cleverly, strapping them under the dragon's wings so the passengers could help themselves. Dirus could use his long blue tongue to siphon off a drink whenever he wanted.

Harry shook hands all around for the last time.

"You come back and see old Harry," he said to Toody. "You too, young Falcon. Those are some fair dinkum kids you've got there, Dr. Peter Davies," he said. "Some kids."

Peter grinned. "Too right, Harry," he said. "Some *fine* kids."

Harry gave the tanks a final tug. "There you go, yer honor," he said, climbing down off Dirus's back.

"Tanks very much," said Dirus, who was so pleased with his pun that he shook with laughter for several minutes.

"I'd stay away from that pawpaw juice, yer honor," said Harry. "You bein' inclined to heartburn, begging yer pardon."

Blinda conjured up a packet of antacid tablets the size of manhole covers for the dragon to chew. They were labeled DRAGAMET and Dirus crunched one up with great enjoyment before they took off. "Mmm, mackerel-mint— my favorite," he said, smacking his lips.

Dirus gathered himself and began chugging across the sand, slowly gaining speed, with the earth shaking under his heavy tread. He left the ground just before he reached the edge of the sea, and Harry and his tribe watched and waved as Dirus skimmed over the surf and flew toward the sun.

CHAPTER
SIXTEEN

THE TRIP HOME WAS NOT NEARLY AS TEDIOUS AS THE trip out. It was very pleasant to sail through the air on the back of a large and temperate dragon. Blinda showed them how to stretch out between the bony struts of Dirus's wings, and they spent the journey lounging there, watching dolphins play in the waves far below.

Unfortunately, what Harry and Blinda hadn't reckoned on was combinations. If Dirus had stuck with cappuccino, Dragamet, and the zwieback Harry had provided, everything would have been hunky-dory, but when the others began eating lunch around half-past eleven (they had had a very early breakfast), the dragon naturally wanted to join them. Harry planned to expand the café, so he had dreamed up all sorts of tempting things to add to the menu. There were avocado sandwiches with sun-dried tomatoes in olive oil on whole wheat; hot pastrami with grilled onions on a rye roll; smoked bluefish with red onions and goat cheese on pita; liverwurst with muenster and scallions on pumpernickel; and Toody's invention, peanut butter, apple, and bacon on white. A big basket of freshly made potato chips, deliciously crunchy and still warm, hung from the dragon's crest, next to a bag of homemade fudge. Everybody ate quite a lot, and Dirus ate most of all, finishing up by polishing off the remains of Toody's and St. George's sandwiches (they didn't like crusts). Blinda watched him with some anxiety as he washed it all down with a long swig of pawpaw juice and a much longer one of cappuccino. "You might want to go easy there, Dirus," she said. "You know what happened before with Mount Saint Hel—" A sudden jolt shook them and everyone grabbed onto a nearby scale and sat up.

"I say!" said St. George. "Easy there, old thing. Bit of unnecessary turbulence, what?"

The dragon swallowed the last of a Dragamet tablet and didn't answer. Falcon looked at Dirus and had the peculiar feeling that if the dragon's face hadn't already been green it would have *turned* green. "Are you all right?" she asked.

Toody, who had some experience with tummy aches, peered closely at Dirus. "You gonna throw up?" he asked. The dragon did not reply.

Faintly at first, so they hardly felt it, a low rumble began to build deep in Dirus's insides. His hide twitched and rippled, growing hotter as the red glow around his heart began to spread, and his whole chest and belly turned bright orange. His passengers began to feel an uncomfortable warmth under their bottoms.

"Hold on tight!" said Blinda. "I think he's going to BLOW!"

She spoke just in the nick of time, for just as everyone grabbed onto the nearest scale there was another jolt and another, and poor Dirus bucked and writhed beneath them, losing altitude rapidly till they felt sea spray on their faces.

Just as Falcon thought they would plunge into the waves, the dragon gave one final buck and a tremendous explosion shattered the air and blasted the clouds to smithereens. A huge jet of purplish green smoke shot out of the dragon's behind, sending them high into the sky with the sound of a thousand trumpets.

Luckily for his passengers, they had a good headwind, so the enormous cloud of stinking gas blew away behind them toward the east. If they had not escaped it, they would surely have died, for even the faint whiff they caught nearly overwhelmed them. It was a foul and fearsome combination of avocado, pastrami, chili peppers, onions, bananas, bluefish, peanut butter, liverwurst, pawpaw, and never-ending cappuccino.

"PEE-YOO!" said Toody, coughing. "You should say 'excuse me'!"

"I do," said Dirus, turning blue with shame. "Oh, I do, I do."

Fortunately they suffered no serious aftereffects,

though all the color was bleached out of their clothing and one of the saint's eyebrows turned bright green, giving him an oddly festive look. The effect on the environment was more dramatic. All the sea birds in the area laid purple eggs that year, and over China, where the fart ended up, the sunsets were spectacular for weeks. The following year a number of Chinese children were born with a small, dragon-shaped birthmark, which, since it happened to be the Year of the Dragon in the Chinese calendar, was considered to be extremely lucky. Quite a few other people got dragon tattoos, but you could always recognize the real birthmarks because they smelled faintly of pastrami.

After that the voyage was uneventful and they amused themselves by singing rounds. Once Dirus had recovered from his embarrassment, he joined in, and as he was the best (and loudest) singer, they sounded quite grand.

By two o'clock they were flying over the Rockies, and at last they saw the towers of New York City glinting in the golden light of the late afternoon sun.

"Drop me off at the Second Avenue Deli, will you, old thing?" said St. George. He kissed Blinda's hand, shook hands solemnly with Toody and Peter, and then reached into his tracksuit and pulled out a small brooch, a red enamel dragon over the words *"Saltare cum draconis"* on a cross of gold attached to a blue and green ribbon. He pinned it on Falcon's collar.

"The Cross of Saint George," he said. "For valor and musical skill in the face of murderous pomposity, I, Saint

George, do declare you, Emily Falcon Davies, to be a true Knight of the Dragon, herewith, howsomever, and etcetera, so on and so forth, tiddle-dee-pom." He kissed her on both cheeks and peered over the edge of Dirus's wing to the streets below. "Just here is fine, old bean. Cheerio!" he said, and stepped off into space.

Falcon gasped in horror, but instead of smashing onto Second Avenue, the saint simply floated down in a dignified way, arms folded across his chest, and landed right in front of the deli. He strode inside muttering, "Maybe some herring salad, too . . ."

Dirus banked west and headed north, and soon they found themselves in sight of the familiar red towers of the Museum of Natural History.

"Land on the Columbus Avenue side," said Blinda, who was an incorrigible back-seat driver. "There's just enough room."

"Not enough to take off again," said Dirus. "And then what'll I do, with all the people coming home from work? I thought I'd head for the Great Lawn."

"I'll help," said Blinda. "I have an antigravity spell right here in this pocket—no, this one. Here it is." She pulled a pink Post-it Note out of her left back pocket, peered at it, held out her hand, and said, "Anti-Newtonian, not Babylonian, oopsy kapoopsy wopple-a-poppullus!" A strange round object appeared in her hand.

"What's that?" asked Toody. The fruit, if that's what it was, was white and juicy like the flesh of an apple, dotted with small dark seeds.

"It's an inside-out-upside-down-backwards apple. Newton's apple fell down, this one falls up," said Blinda.

"Won't it give me gas?" said Dirus, eyeing the fruit anxiously.

"Not so you'll notice," said Blinda. The dragon circled the museum and made a perfect five-point landing on the lawn in front of the planetarium.

"Now then," said Blinda. "Get along, you three. Missy's waiting."

"Will we see you again?" asked Falcon.

Blinda smoothed a stray lock of hair off Falcon's forehead. "So like your Great-Great-Aunt Emily," she said. "You'll not have an easy life, m'dear, but it'll never be dull." She smiled. "Courage, laughter, and comfortable shoes, that's the ticket. And tea any afternoon, when I'm in town," said the witch. "Half-past three and welcome." She hugged them all. "You come, too, and bring Missy," she said to Peter, who thanked her for the invitation. Falcon wrapped her arms as far as they would go around Dirus's scaly neck.

"Thank you for . . . for everything. Where will you go now?"

The dragon shook his head, splattering Falcon with lilac-scented tears. "Dear, oh dearie me, I hate to say goodbye. . . . I expect I'll join Egg in Parallel New York. It's time she learned some proper poetry from an expert. I think I'll skip that apple, though, and have a bit of a rest first, if Ms. Cholmondely here can shrink me a bit?"

"Oh, yes indeed," said the witch. "Now let's see, how

131

does it go? Waggy baggy diddle? No, that's for wrinkles. Yorka porka? Samma sooma?" Falcon and Toody hugged them one last time and stood back as Blinda began to chant, "Hagga dagga boo, flew, flo, flied. Twelve-yard dragons are hard to hide. Twirl around and thrice times blink—Dirus Horribilus, you shall SHRINK!"

Blinda twirled around and blinked three times, and to Falcon's amazement, Dirus, with a squealing sound like air coming out of a balloon, shrank rapidly until he was no bigger than a kitten. Several people on their way home from work rubbed their eyes and sighed. "Working too hard," they muttered. "For a minute, I thought I saw a flying dinosaur there by the museum. Got to slow down, take it easy."

The tiny dragon waved his foreleg at Toody and Falcon.

"Au revoir but not goodbye. Dare and do, and don't just try. Come for tea and let's be merry, Falcon, girl extraordinary," he squeaked.

Blinda picked him up and slipped him into her largest pocket, and with a wave of her hand she marched off to the bus stop just as a number 10 pulled up on Central Park West.

Falcon, Toody, and Peter watched as Blinda climbed aboard and rode off down Central Park West to the magical house on Charles Street. Falcon stretched, arching her back like a cat, and looked around at the museum's red towers and Central Park all green with spring. It was good to know there was a genuine certified witch not far away, and the world so full of possibilities. Peter straightened the medal on her collar. "Girl extraordinary," he said, putting his arm around her shoulders. She looked down at her brother.

"*Boy* extraordinary," she said, and Toody took her hand.

"Can we go see Missy *now?*" he said.

"Yes, we can," said Falcon. "Let's go home!"

There are two fake quotations in this book. Can you find them?

GLOSSARY

Mangled Shakespeare, Euripides, and Eliot, mended

PAGE 30:
A Midsummer Night's Dream, Act II, Scene I
"Ill met by moonlight, proud Titania." (Oberon)

PAGE 31:
As You Like It, Act II, Scene IV
"When I was at home, I was in a better place:
but travellers must be content." (Touchstone)

The Life of King Henry the Fifth, Act III, Scene I
"Once more unto the breach, dear friends,
once more; or close the wall up with our English dead!"
(King Henry V)

PAGE 34:
The Tempest, Act V, Epilogue
"Let me not,
Since I have my dukedom got
And pardon'd the deceiver, dwell
In this bare island by your spell;
But release me from my bands
With the help of your good hands." (Prospero)

The Tempest, Act I, Scene II
"Come unto these yellow sands,
And then take hands." (Ariel)

Ion by Euripides
"I shall carry out the task assigned me.
Come, old foot, become young in deeds in spite of the years."
(Old Retainer)

Troilus and Cressida, Act II, Scene III
"A stirring dwarf we do allowance give
Before a sleeping giant. . . ." (Agamemnon)

Hamlet, Prince of Denmark, Act III, Scene IV
"Upon the heat and flame of thy distemper
Sprinkle cool patience." (Queen)

A Midsummer Night's Dream, Act III, Scene II
"And sleep, that sometimes shuts up sorrow's eye." (Helena)

The First Part of King Henry the Fourth, Act III, Scene I
"I can call spirits from the vasty deep." (Glendower)
"Why, so can I, or so can any man;
But will they come when you do call for them?"
(Hotspur)

The Life of King Henry the Fifth, Act IV, Scene III
"All things are ready, if our minds be so." (King Henry)

The Third Part of King Henry the Sixth, Act III, Scene III
"Yield not thy neck
To fortune's yoke, but let thy dauntless mind
Still ride in triumph over all mischance." (King Lewis)

Cymbeline, Act III, Scene I
"Let proof speak." (Lucius)

Pericles, Prince of Tyre, Act III, Scene I
"For truth can never be confirm'd enough,
Though doubts did ever sleep." (Pericles)

"The Love Song of J. Alfred Prufrock" by T. S. Eliot
"I grow old . . . I grow old . . .
I shall wear the bottoms of my trousers rolled."

All's Well That Ends Well, Act V, Scene III
"Oft our displeasures, to ourselves unjust,
Destroy our friends and after weep their dust. . . ." (King)

The Taming of the Shrew, Act III, Scene II
"I will be master of what is mine own." (Petruchio)

Hamlet, Prince of Denmark, Act IV, Scene V
"When sorrows come, they come not single spies
But in battalions." (King)

Richard III, Act IV, Scene IV
"Look, what is done cannot be now amended:
Men shall deal unadvisedly sometimes,
Which after-hours give leisure to repent." (King Richard)

Timon of Athens, Act III, Scene V
"What folly 'tis to hazard life for ill!" (First Senator)

The Life of King Henry the Fifth, Act IV, Scene III
"We few, we happy few, we band of brothers. . . ."
(King Henry)

Julius Caesar, Act I, Scene II
"Yond Cassius has a lean and hungry look;
He thinks too much. Such men are dangerous." (Caesar)

What Folly Spent 3.2.18
"I fear your ardor be so hot
That it may but yourself consume,
Or passion's flame be unallayed,
You will forseek a gallet's tomb." (Jocatia)

The Second Part of King Henry the Sixth, Act II, Scene I
"God's goodness hath been great to thee . . .
But still remember what the Lord hath done."
(King Henry)

Page 120:
Measure for Measure, Act I, Scene III
"So our decrees,
Dead to infliction, to themselves are dead,
And liberty plucks justice by the nose." (Duke)

PAGE 121:
The Two Gentlemen of Verona, Act II, Scene VII
"A true-devoted pilgrim is not weary
To measure kingdoms with his feeble steps. . . ." (Julia)

Julius Caesar, Act IV, Scene III
"On such a full sea are we now afloat;
And we must take the current when it serves,
Or lose our ventures." (Brutus)

PAGE 122:
Romeo and Juliet, Act II, Scene II
"Good-night, good-night! Parting is such sweet sorrow
That I shall say good-night till it be morrow." (Juliet)

The Tragedy of Macbeth, Act I, Scene I
"When shall we three meet again
In thunder, lightning, or in rain?" (First Witch)

Note: Different editions of Shakespeare's plays will have differences in the text.

BLINDA'S
OATMEAL CRUNCH
COOKIES

Makes about 3¹/₂ dozen cookies

Preheat oven to 350 degrees.

In a large bowl, combine:

2 cups old-fashioned rolled oats	*³/₄ teaspoon baking powder*
1 ¹/₂ cups Grape Nuts cereal	*¹/₂ teaspoon salt*
1 ³/₄ cups whole wheat flour	*³/₄ teaspoon cinnamon*
³/₄ teaspoon baking soda	*¹/₂ teaspoon nutmeg*

In a large bowl or mixer bowl, combine and beat until blended:

2 sticks (¹/₂ lb.) unsalted butter	*¹/₄ cup sugar*
* at room temperature*	*2 large eggs*
1¹/₂ cups dark brown sugar	*1 tablespoon vanilla extract*
* (packed)*	

Add oatmeal mixture to butter mixture and stir just until well blended. Scoop by tablespoonfuls onto cookie sheets that have been greased or lined with parchment paper and bake 10 to 12 minutes, or until golden brown. Let stand about 2 minutes after removing from oven and carefully loosen cookies with a spatula. (If they cool off too much and stick to the cookie sheet, put them back in the oven for a minute or two.) Cool on a rack and enjoy with your favorite witch.